# STINGRAY

## You Can't Hide Forever

### By

### Gary Zeiger

TholianWeb Productions
Jacksonville, FL

First Edition Text Copyright ©2011 by Gary Zeiger
Second Edition Text Copyright ©2020 by Gary Zeiger
www.GaryZeiger.com

First Edition Illustrations and Cover Design by Charles Sutton
Copyright ©2011 by TholianWeb Productions, Inc.

Second Edition Cover Design by Manuel Silva
Copyright ©2020 by TholianWeb Productions, Inc.

Published by TholianWeb Productions, Inc.
www.TholianWebPublishing.com

Library of Congress Cataloging-in-Publication Data Available

Library of Congress Control Number: 2011941691

ISBN 978-1-935852-09-4 (print edition)
ISBN 978-1-935852-10-0 (eBook edition)

First Edition: November 2011
Second Edition: June 2020

10 9 8 7 6 5 4 3 2 1

<u>SPECIAL THANKS TO</u>:


My Wife, Tonya
*for putting up with all my cockamamie ideas over the years!*

Dave Seay, LCDR, USN Retired
*for keeping my naval and nautical terms ship-shape.*

# CHAPTER ONE

Captain Reginald Franklin Epsilon was the former captain of the AWS *Freedom*. The *Freedom* was the flagship of the Alliance Of Arms (AOA) which had been the military branch of the Planetary Alliance. The Planetary Alliance was a union of planets throughout the known universe who had aligned together for common trade and protection. Eps, as his friends called him, was trudging through the snow, carrying a stack of cut firewood on his back. He was ruggedly handsome, average height, muscular build, and looked to be in his late thirties to early forties. His eyes were dark and piercing, and his brown hair was somewhat spiky. Today he was sporting a full beard, which was something he hadn't done in a very long time. He came from a line of military and pirate men, all with mysterious lives.

At his side was his trusty friend Timber, half Alaskan Malamute and half Siberian Husky. Eps never found a better breed of dog, even through his extensive travels as an Alliance star cruiser captain. He got Timber as a puppy three years ago from Taliriktug, one of only two real friends he could completely trust. Tal came from a long line of Inuit dog breeders and was first generation Inuit to move off planet and continue to breed this fine dog. The Conglomerate blockade of Earth put a strain on his ability to breed the Malamute/Husky combo, though he still maintained connections that were willing to supply stock, for a premium fee of course. When asked how he got his name, he joked that his mother had a fiery sense of humor. In Inuit, Taliriktug meant "strong arm". She complained that he was constantly punching her while he was inside her womb and would say that the boy was trying to get out. The irony was that when he was born, he literally popped right out, but with only one arm!

Epsilon was returning to the cabin he built from the surrounding trees. The wood was much harder than trees on other planets (it had to be to survive in this constant cold) and, as a result, it afforded better insulation from the weather. Once it started to burn, it would burn hotter and longer than other woods. Eps made a point of not using technology, afraid its use could tip off the Conglomerate Military Command (CMC) to his position. However, for cutting and chopping this wood, the only tool that would cut this stuff was a laser hand saw. He and Timber were the only life forms on this planet. The indigenous life died out many decades ago due to this system's sun decaying. The planet was on the edge of the Frontier and so far removed from civilization that it didn't have a name, nor was it on any star map. It was a perfect place to hide.

The governments of the Planetary Alliance were duped (as Eps would put it) into believing that a group of corporations (calling itself "The Conglomerate") could run their respective governments better and cheaper. The "people" would benefit in the long run with more services, less waste, and no wars. Leading this charge for change was President Amabo Karab, a sweet talking used shuttle craft salesman. So, one-by-one, each planet voted to join the Conglomerate and dissolve their government in favor of corporate rule. The Conglomerate also acquired each of the fallen government's resources, including their military. As each planet fell victim, the Conglomerate amassed a vast military armada, which came under the purview of the CMC.

One planet refused to give in. The people of this planet had already experienced the promised "change" by politician after politician. Earth knew what was in store and stood alone against the Conglomerate. She recalled all of her ambassadors and citizens living abroad along with her extensive military forces and entered into a period of semi-isolationism. Earth still traded with other planets, though it was mostly resistance freedom fighters that ran the Conglomerate blockade set up around Earth. Even with all the military might combined from the old Planetary Alliance, Earth's forces could easily defeat them. The Conglomerate's attempt to starve the people of Earth was feeble at best. She's a survivor.

\* \* \*

Today was an unusually cold and dim day. Wisps of an asteroid belt could be seen in the sky moving between the planet and what feeble sun this system still had. According to his scans when he first arrived, the sun was burning out. He estimated another couple of years before he and Timber would have to find a new residence. *I think a warmer planet next time.*

Epsilon dumped his chopped wood on the front porch by the door and opened it. He watched as Timber immediately ran in and curled up by the fire.

"Wuss," he said to the dog who sighed and closed his eyes, as Epsilon shut the door. He looked out the window and saw that it was snowing—again. "Well, fella, looks like we're in for another snowstorm." Timber grunted as he rolled over to warm his belly, ignoring his friend. Eps just shook his head.

Looking around his one-room cabin, it was modestly furnished. Most everything had been scavenged from different space vessels that met their demise and were left drifting lifelessly in space. In the far corner was the fireplace which was fashioned out of a boiler from a cruise liner, her long gone guests no longer required hot water. A bunk taken from a frigate sat next to it. A window over the bunk looked out at an expanse of nothing but snow and more snow. The back wall had no windows since it backed up to a solid wall of ice that was several kilometers thick. There was a collection of tools and weapons hanging on it. One of his favorites was an old, very rare Smith & Wesson Model 29 .44 Magnum revolver. He'd acquired it, along with several cans of ammunition, at a jockey lot on Gamma Carlos Prime for a song.

Actually, he "handled" some thugs that were shaking down the vendors in the lot. As a token, one of the grateful vendors gave it to him.

At the other end of the cabin was the kitchen. Honestly, it was nothing more than a place to store and prepare food, as the cooking was done in the fireplace over the open fire. When they arrived on the planet, Eps brought enough protein to last them for two years. In the forest, he found local roots and fruits, which he surmised nature had intended for her long-deceased inhabitants. Using these, he was able to extend their food supply an additional year. In the coming months he will be forced to go off planet to resupply his food stock, a risky trip that he is not looking forward to. There were two windows here that looked out onto rows and rows of trees. The trees were very tall, standing some thirty to fifty meters. Their trunks were some ten meters in girth and bare until the top, which blossomed into thousands and thousands of thin green spikes. The bark was rough with a reddish-brown color to it.

The front wall had the only door to the cabin as well as three windows that looked out across another vast expanse of snow. The only vegetation that could be seen was the forest to the left. Under the front windows was a real couch, taken from some wealthy aristocrat's doomed vessel. Finally, in the middle of the room was a table with two chairs, also taken from that same lavish vessel, with both place settings set; like a dinner guest was expected at any moment.

Taking another glance around the room, you couldn't help but notice that the windows were a Hodge-Podge, taken from different types of vessels. Looking again at the back wall, the eye was drawn to a box mounted high up on the wall near the kitchen. The nondescript metallic box had one red protruding lamp centered on the top. The front face near the top contained a round screen, the middle face held what appeared to be a small, round speaker and the bottom face had a couple of switches and a round glass piece. It looked like something out of a 1960s era nuclear missile launch facility on Earth.

Capt. Epsilon never visited Earth. He was captivated by all

of the wonderful stories and tales that had been passed from one ship to another over the years: About the first ships that sailed the seas and were attacked by monsters from the deep; the birth of the United States of America and then on to her Industrial Revolution; the romance of pre-Castro Cuba; the rise and fall of Communism in Russia; the first space flight of the Apollo missions (HE didn't count popping up into orbit then coming back down as space flight); the building of the first planetary space station orbiting Earth and then on to the first space port built on the moon; and finally, the first interstellar space flight by astronaut Capt. Reginald Franklin Epsilon (Eps's "Great-something" Grandfather) and cosmonaut Ivan Koblista. Their accomplishment was achieved by using an early form of the modern-day hyper-drive. During that historic flight, the space travelers made another unprecedented discovery: contact with an alien species. This set into rapid motion Earth's launch into space politics. This would set the standards for inter-species relations and government, culminating in the formation of the Planetary Alliance. There was much speculation among the conspiracy theorists of the time of how Earth obtained hyper-drive technology in the first place and who the senior Capt. Epsilon really was. Decades later, it was revealed that there was indeed a cover up as the senior Capt. Epsilon was not actually born on Earth. There was no mention, however, of where he was from and shortly after returning to Earth, he mysteriously vanished. It was widely speculated that he was gallivanting around the universe with the aliens he introduced to Earth during his first contact. Unfortunately, the species, known as the Corrallans, was now extinct due to a virus outbreak. Cosmonaut Koblista never expounded publicly on what he put into his official report. That report remains highly classified even until today while Koblista took whatever secrets he had to his grave.

The romance of Earth had truly captivated Eps. He thoroughly studied her people and what they did right (and what they did wrong) throughout the centuries. He put this research to use during his life to stay one step ahead of every situation; that and his unique lineage, which is something he has gone to great lengths to keep secret.

* * *

As Epsilon prepared dinner, Timber's ears perked up, and he started to howl. He got up and nervously circled the cabin a couple of times, whining and growling. Looking straight up, he let out a deep, loud howl. As if on cue, the red light atop the little metal box started blinking. The little screen came to life, showing a lone dot halfway from the edge and moving toward the center.

"WARNING!" blared a female voice out of the little speaker on the front of the box. "Incoming unidentified vessel. Time to orbit: one minute."

"Well, Timber, both of you need your early warning detection systems overhauled," Epsilon exclaimed, as he hit the silence button on the box. The red light continued to flash, and the screen showed the approach of the vessel.

"WARNING!" blared the box again a short time later. "Unidentified vessel entering atmosphere. Time to intercept: one minute." At that, Timber started howling again, this time looking straight at the door.

"Great," Epsilon said. "Probably some moron trying to sell entertainment subscriptions." Timber emitted a low growl and laid down in front of the door. Epsilon grabbed his .44 Magnum, strapped it to his waist and looked out the window as a small transport ship hovered about three meters above the snow and about a half klick (kilometer) away.

A door on the side of the ship opened and out dropped what looked like a person into the snow. As fast as it arrived, it was gone. "Ooo, that's gonna leave a mark," Epsilon said to Timber. He watched the being stagger up, try to walk toward the cabin, and fall down again. Something looked familiar about that being, but Epsilon just couldn't put his finger on it. "Hmm," he muttered. "That ship is pretty small to be this far out with no support vessel," he said, to no one in particular, while looking at the lone dot retreating on the scope. He grabbed the door handle with one hand and the scruff of Timber's neck with the other. While opening the door, he said, "Go bring 'em back, boy," and released the hound.

With a hearty "WOOF," Timber was off after the intruder, his mighty legs gobbled up the distance with ease and speed, reaching the intruder in no time. Grabbing the shirt collar with his mouth, he started dragging the being back toward the cabin. About halfway to the cabin, the being, a human female, finally stood up and started walking. *Ah, I wondered when she would show up.*

* * *

The wet and cold woman came through the cabin door, wearing only a ragged Conglomerate uniform shirt, pants, and no shoes. Epsilon ushered her immediately into the cabin and in front of the fire.

Teeth chattering, she emitted a meek, "Hi Eps. Sorry I haven't come by sooner." The woman was none other than Lt. Jessie Smythe, former XO (Executive, or First, Officer) of the AWS *Freedom*, previously under his command. Epsilon was always fond of Jess and took her under his wing as his protégé.

"I was beginning to think you had forgotten about me, Jess," Epsilon responded, as Timber sniffed the newcomer up and down. Satisfied, he jumped up on the bed, curled up in a ball, and nodded off.

"You're a hard guy to find," she chattered, as Epsilon took a hand-held scanner out of a box on the floor and set it on the mantel over the fireplace.

"Well, what can I say? There are some who would have my head for no good reason."

"Never thought I'd see you sporting a full beard."

"Well, in case you hadn't noticed, it's a wee bit chilly outside. Helps keep from getting frostbite."

"Expecting someone?" she asked, nodding toward the table.

"Ah yes, I was hoping you'd drop by for dinner some time!" Epsilon pulled some clothes and a towel out of another box on the floor. "Here, take off those wet clothes and put these on," he commanded, as he tossed the clothes on the corner of the bed.

"They want *Stingray* back, Eps," Jess stated, matter-of-factly, as she turned her back toward Epsilon, faced the fire, and stripped off all her wet clothes.

"First off, I don't have *Stingray*." He grabbed her arm, stopping her from reaching for the towel. She stood there, facing the fire, completely naked. She hadn't changed a bit in the three years since he had seen her last. She still had a rock-hard body, curvy hips, firm buttocks, and a set of legs that would stop any man dead in their tracks. Her disheveled, long, brown hair came down to her mid-back and was not tied up in its usual ponytail. Still facing the fire, he held her in front of him and grabbed the scanner. He let go of her arm and snatched her hair. Moving it aside, he started scanning her neck, arms, and shoulders. Bingo, a red dot appeared on her right shoulder blade. Pressing the red button on the scanner, a red beam of light jumped out and cut her smooth, silky skin. Jess always had a high tolerance for pain, showing only the slightest trace of a wince as she bit her lip. Letting go of her hair, Epsilon pulled the transmitter/tracker from her shoulder with a pair of tweezers and put it on the mantel. Pressing the green button, a thick, green beam erupted forth, and he waved it over the incision. When finished, there was no trace that a cut had ever been made.

Continuing with the scan, he swept it down her back, past the small of her back, to the top of her perfect buttocks. Another red dot appeared on the top of her right cheek. He performed the incision, removal and repair and placed the device on the mantel. He continued down passing her tight cheeks and onto those long, gorgeous legs of hers.

Straightening back up, he grabbed her arm and twirled her around and looked deep into those mesmerizing green eyes. She made no move to cover herself up. Epsilon scanned down her neck, chest and over those naturally firm, large breasts. Not too large, but just right for her build. Continuing down her stomach and past her belly button, another red dot appeared just above her pubic area. He performed the incision, removal, and repair, and again he placed the "bug" on the mantel. As he continued scanning down the front of both of those stunning legs, he remembered being back on the *Freedom* and stealing glances at those legs when they were in the gym. Today, though, she was quite hairy from her waist down, well out of character for her.

"Secondly, who are 'they'?" he asked, convinced she was now bug free. He handed her the towel and clothes and turned around, finally giving her some privacy.

"'They' are the CMC, specifically Admiral Roth," she said. "And he is hell bent on getting *Stingray* back from you. They really made you out to be a ruthless villain. They tagged you for blowing up that research station, killing hundreds of men, women and children from several races and stealing *Stingray*, their newest ship that they claimed they were building for peaceful exploration and humanitarian support."

"Well, it wasn't me. I don't have *Stingray*. Besides, everyone knows that *Stingray* was a state-of-the-art warship that the Conglomerate would be more than happy to unleash on Earth or any other planet that dared to challenge its authority. Who do they think they're fooling? I applaud whoever destroyed it!"

"Roth has Maggie, Eps. He'll trade. Maggie for *Stingray*," she blurted out, on the verge of tears. Epsilon knew Jess well enough to know that she wasn't acting. He had never, in the three plus years she served with him, seen her cry, or even come close to tears. She turned away and wiped her eyes with the shirt Epsilon gave her. "CMC Secret Service agents stormed my village. Mom and Dad were killed in the scuffle trying to protect Mags. They burned the house to the ground. They shot quite a few villagers who tried to intervene."

"Where is he holding your sister?" Epsilon asked, with sincerity in his voice, the commanding tone gone. He had met Maggie a couple times when Jess invited him to spend shore leave with her at her home on Varguti. Maggie took to him immediately and was adamant that one day she would marry him. They all laughed, but out of the corner of his eye, Epsilon had caught the "back off" look Jess gave her little sister.

"Prison-12 on Cammamu," she said, deflated. A chill ran down Epsilon's spine as his eyes meet Jess's. Prison-12 housed political prisoners. No visitors. No oversight. Torture was a common practice. It was said that was where interrogators were trained. Female prisoners were routinely raped for the fun and pleasure of the guards. It was a despicable place, and Maggie was as good as dead if she was even still alive.

"How do you know she's still alive?"

"I've spoken to her. She said that they were hard on her, but so far hadn't hurt her too much. She's in an area set aside for 'special' inmates. Roth said the warden is under his strict orders to make sure she stays pure, so long as I cooperate. I'm sorry, Reg. I had no choice. Please give them *Stingray* back. Maggie loves you; you know that!" Jess pleaded.

Aside from his military commanders, only two other people were allowed to address him by his given name, or any derivative thereof, without riling him up and Jess was one of them. Otherwise, it usually ended in an all-out fistfight. "I'm sorry Jess, there's nothing I can do." He had never seen a defeated look in her eyes before. It hurt him to the core. He couldn't believe the Conglomerate would stoop that low to kill an officer's parents and kidnap her sister.

Timber started to howl, and Epsilon knew what that meant. Grabbing the transmitters, he threw them into the hot fire. Three loud pops meant that they were no longer sending their conversation back to Roth. The red light on the metal box started to flash.

"WARNING!" emanated from the speaker. "Multiple Conglomerate warships approaching. Within firing range in 10 minutes."

"What the—" Jess exclaimed. It was her voice coming from the speaker.

"I missed you, OKAY?" he said, pressing the silence button on the box. He then flipped up the red cap and pushed the old-fashioned toggle switch to the up position.

"Identify!" Jess's voice exclaimed from the box. Epsilon

pressed his face to the box, and it scanned his retina. "Identity Confirmed. Enter command!" the box said.

He stood back. "Go to DEFCON ONE."

"DEFCON ONE set. Confirm!" Epsilon toggled the switch down and closed the cap. "DEFCON ONE is confirmed. T-Minus fifteen minutes and counting!"

The approaching dots on the screen were replaced with the minutes and seconds counting down. DEFCON was the old "DEFense CONdition" readiness scale used by NATO (North Atlantic Treaty Organization) during the Cold War era between the United States and Russia on Earth. DEFCON ONE meant war!

"I suggest we don't dally, my dear," Epsilon said, as he banged three times on the wall below the box. A hidden panel opened, revealing a wall of ice and a large hole in it. Securing the panel in the open position, he hoisted Timber up and fed him into the hole. "Ladies next," he said to Jess, pushing her toward the hole.

"Whoa, there!" she protested. "Where does that go? You know I hate tunnels. YOU hate tunnels!"

"You have a choice. In the hole and live or stay here and die along with Maggie. Besides, have I ever led you astray?" He smiled at her and catching her off guard, grabbed her and thrust her into the hole head-first. Jumping in feet-first, he pulled the panel shut behind him and the hatch once again became hidden. All that was left was an empty, quiet cabin and the crackling sounds of the fire. This was the calm before the storm.

* * *

The box was wrong. They arrived sooner than it said they would. Three CMC warships popped out of hyper-space, two of them assumed a standard orbit and the third one took up a higher combat position. One of the ships' bellies opened up and two large transport shuttles emerged and sped to the planet's surface.

* * *

The two shuttles hovered a few meters above the packed snow, about a klick out from the cabin. Two platoons of soldiers jumped from the shuttles and fanned out as they approached the cabin. Row upon row of CMC Marines advanced upon their target. Roth was no fool; he knew taking Epsilon wouldn't be easy. His sub-commanders raised their eyebrows when he ordered that many Marines to apprehend one man: by himself, on a desolate planet. Little did they know that was when Captain Epsilon was the most dangerous. As the troops advanced to within a half klick of the cabin, three M60Q5 machine guns swung down from the ceiling of the porch. These, plus ten thousand rounds of ammunition for each gun, were additional gems Eps picked up from that same jockey lot. He really liked the simplicity of the setup. The Q5 edition was a mounted unit with old school sensors to track targets: radar (radio waves bounced off the target) and infrared (detectors that sensed heat). The system was controlled by an isolated onboard targeting and tracking computer. Essentially, it was hack proof (at least in the short amount of time that it would run while defending the cabin). The guns swiveled from side to side, acquired their targets and opened fire. Somewhere in the antiquated electronics something short-circuited, probably due to the intense cold. Instead of acquiring a target, firing a short burst, acquiring another target, firing, and repeating, the guns opened up. Sweeping back and forth, they mowed down soldier after soldier, row after row. CMC gunners on the open decks of the shuttles fired their mounted laser cannons at the cabin, but the cabin's shields absorbed the laser blasts. Several rounds from one of the M60's hit the gunner on one of the shuttles as he was firing, causing him to spin around. Still squeezing the trigger, he obliterated his own flight crew. With no driver, the shuttle started spinning out of control. It dove head-first into the other shuttle, whose pilot didn't notice the approaching shuttle until it was too late. Both shuttles erupted into huge balls of fire and dropped out of the sky onto several rows of Marines who had no time to react.

Ten thousand rounds may seem like a lot of projectiles for

a weapon; however, since they were running non-stop and firing twelve hundred rounds per minute, they ran out of ammunition in just over eight minutes. The ensuing silence was only broken by the occasional moan from a downed marine and the burning shuttle wreckage. The pristine white snow turned crimson with the spilled blood of the soldiers. There were only a handful of survivors and realizing they were the only ones left, they opened up on the cabin with their laser rifles, but the shield once again absorbed their laser fire. The continued barrage along with the weakening from the big guns, though, overloaded the shield generator and it exploded in a shower of sparks. The couch inside the cabin erupted in flames since the shield generator was located underneath it.

The half-dozen marines charged the cabin, leaping over their dead and bloodied comrades. Jumping onto the porch, they didn't miss a stride as they collided with the door, broke it off its mount, and spilled into the cabin. It was empty. The only sounds were coming from the crackling of the fires and Jess's recorded voice: "ten, nine, eight, seven, six...."

"OH SHIT!" yelled one of the Marines, as they all turned on their heels to run out the door. As they would soon find out, running wouldn't save them.

## CHAPTER TWO

After a short, but very fast, descent through the ice tube, Timber, Jess and Eps emerged into a dark, cold, chamber. "Lights!" Epsilon exclaimed, and the chamber lit up brightly, revealing a small cavern. The walls, floor and ceiling were all frosted white ice. "Computer, execute emergency protocol alpha!" The computer beeped twice, and a thick sheet of ice dropped, sealing the hole they just came through. They heard a whirring sound as electronic equipment started powering up.

During their descent they heard the "thump-thump-thump" of the guns blazing. Now, standing in the middle of the cave, they continued to hear the muffled gunfire of the MQ60's thirty meters or so above them.

Jess noticed that there was a single console at one end of the cave and a platform at the other end. "You have transporter capability!" she exclaimed. "I'd heard rumors that it was under development."

"It works, now get into one of those pressure suits," Eps responded, motioning to the wall behind the platform. Hanging there were three pressure suits, and on the floor below them was a pressurized kennel. Two of the suits were in Epsilon's size and the other smaller one was in Jess's size.

"You were expecting me," Jess mumbled to herself, as she slid on her suit.

Eps smiled to himself and pretended to ignore her while he

loaded Timber into the kennel that he placed on the platform, shut its door, and activated its life support system. He then slid on his suit. Turning to Jess, he latched the top ring on her suit and twisted her helmet on. Turning her around, he activated her life support system. Next, he then latched his top ring, twisted on his helmet, and activated his life support.

"Can you hear me Jess?" he asked, over the internal communication system.

"Yes," she responded.

"Good. Get on the platform." Eps headed over to the console and flipped a switch. As he pressed the red button, the whirring got louder, and he jogged over and jumped onto the platform. "Hang on!"

\* \* \*

All of a sudden Jess's whole world turned upside down. A brilliant burst of purple light, then nothing, then more purple light and then darkness.

"OH MY GOD!" Jess exclaimed, as she staggered. "My innards felt like they were being wrenched out of my body."

"Give yourself a burst of cold oxygen and hold your breath a little. It will help with the nausea. You get used to it after a few transports," Eps said, as he pushed a button on his wrist-mounted control pad. Lights came on to reveal an enormous rock cavern. They were standing on a similar looking platform as the one in the ice cavern with a similar looking control panel across from it. Turning around, Jess saw Epsilon pulling Timber's kennel toward a ship, the likes of which she had never seen. "Come on Jess, we don't have much time."

"You do have *Stingray*!" Jess exclaimed. Eps detected the brightness in her voice as she realized there was a ray of hope of getting her sister back alive.

"Sorry about lying to you back in the cabin. It was for the benefit of those listening in."

"Hrmph," she said, and slowly started toward the ship,

obviously in awe. "She's beautiful!"

The ship was gray in color with a round, blunt nose. Rising up from the nose was a hump with two rows of large windows. Facing forward, the top row had a window in the center and one on each side heading toward the back (aft) of the ship. The second row was missing the center window but had the two, though larger, windows that wrapped around to the side. Along the sides, both rows had large portholes, one right after each other, heading aft. Finally, the hump angled down toward the rear of the ship where it fanned out to the left and right, making a large wing that ended in a straight edge on the rear of the ship. Looking at the outside edges of each wing, the edges turned sharply up in a triangular shape with the pointed end facing up and the long edge facing back. On the bottom of the ship from mid-ship to the aft end, another hump protruded with what looked like a hangar door. Jess assumed this to be the cargo hold. Standing at thirty meters tall (not counting the fin tips or the docking clamps holding her to the rock floor), ninety meters long, and a wingspan of forty meters, she was an impressive looking ship.

"Move your ass Smythe!" Epsilon yelled, from an airlock door on the side of the cargo bay "hump."

Breaking out of her trance, she double-timed it toward the entrance ladder. She climbed up the simple metal ladder toward the airlock door, out of which Eps had just stuck his helmeted head. Running over and climbing the ladder was easy as there was hardly any gravity.

"Where are we?" Jess asked.

"We're deep inside the closest moon," Epsilon said, as he pushed the kennel through the door and continued on in. As Jess came through the door, Eps hit a button on a panel next to it and the outer door slid shut. Pressing another button, the inside door slid open, and they went on through. He pressed another button and the inside door slid shut. Since *Stingray* was powered down, there was no pressurization. The entire ship was in vacuum and keeping both airlock doors closed kept dust and debris from floating in.

The only illumination was from their helmet mounted lights. Inside the large cargo bay there were many stacked boxes. As if anticipating her question, Eps motioned towards the containers, "Provisions." Parked in the near and far aft corners of the bay on either side of the hangar door were two shuttle crafts. There was an uncanny resemblance to their mother ship. In the middle of the forward wall was a large door and to its left was yet another control panel and a larger transport platform.

The duo headed through that door, Eps dragging Timber's kennel behind. It opened as they approached and closed after they were through, and they emerged into a main corridor. Wasting no time, they headed up a set of metal stairs to the next level with Eps carrying the kennel and Jess following behind. Turning and heading aft a few feet, they swung around and headed up another set of metal stairs. Their final destination was a dark room. Eps put the kennel down against the wall and pressed a button on his control pad. "Computer, emergency departure protocol."

"Emergency departure protocol activated," the computer responded in the customary mechanical female voice.

"Well, at least you didn't reprogram THIS computer with my voice," Jess said, sarcastically.

The room lit up and the heavy doors they just entered through closed with a thud. It was obvious they were on the command deck. It was *Stingray's* bridge and nerve center. A hissing sounded as the bridge started to pressurize. After a few moments, the computer announced, "Pressurization complete. Confirm identity." Epsilon twisted off his helmet with a whoosh, walked over to a console, and pressed his eye up to the scanner. "Identity confirmed. Emergency departure protocol in-process," barked the computer.

Epsilon took off his gloves and let Timber out of the kennel while Jess removed her helmet and gloves. There were three large windows/screens on the bridge: one facing forward and the other two at slight angles facing left and right, respectively. There were two main consoles up front with chairs in front of them. The command chair sat in the middle on an elevated platform. There were consoles on the left, right and back of the bridge with chairs in front of them as well. Eps sat down in the left front chair and started pressing buttons. Jess sat down in the chair next to him, taking a moment to figure out the controls.

"Okay, sub-light engines are online and ready," Eps announced, pointing to a set of two large sliders, one of which was lit up. "BAM-BAM" came from somewhere port side aft. "Umbilical and ladder jettisoned." Another louder "BOOM" sounded from underneath, causing *Stingray* to shudder and feel as if she was no longer anchored. "Docking clamps released, we are free to maneuver." Eps positioned the ship in front of a section of the rock wall. "Are you ready?" he asked, turning to Jess.

A cold calmness came over Jess as she faced Eps. "Let's dance!"

Nodding, Eps pointed to a button in front of her. "Raise the shields." She pressed it, and a buzzing sounded momentarily in response.

"Shields at one hundred percent," she acknowledged.

Eps pressed a button overhead. In front of them, an oval shape lit up on the rock wall. In the center of the oval shape was a gray circular object.

"Three, two, one," announced the computer. The entire cavern shuddered. While pieces of rock and debris fell onto *Stingray*, her shields protected her from any damage.

"Shields holding at one hundred percent," Jess said.

The oval ring of light had exploded and dislodged a massive piece of rock from the wall. As soon as the rock separated from the rest of the cavern, a bright light emanated from the middle of the rock, shooting a stream of hot gases at *Stingray*. Her shields absorbed it without the slightest hesitation.

"WOW!" Jess exclaimed. The bright light was a massive rocket engine that was propelling the gigantic piece of rock forward, leaving a gaping hole between the cavern and outer space.

Eps started inching *Stingray* forward and through the hole. "The rock has natural properties in it that defeat scanners," Epsilon explained. "Hollowing out the cavern was a piece of cake for

*Stingray's* forward laser cannon. Putting the piece of rock back proved a wee bit of a daunting task for one person though. Using the cannon again on lower power, I sealed the rock together and rigged explosives to break the seam and any ice build-up. The rocket engine that I found in an abandoned ship was the perfect tool for moving it out of the way."

With the piece of rock propelling itself in front of them, *Stingray* emerged into the coldness of space for the first time in almost three years. Fortunately, Lady Luck was on their side for a change. The orbital position of the moon, in relation to the planet and the Conglomerate warships, put the emerging rock and *Stingray* on opposite sides. All of a sudden *Stingray's* sensors came alive!

"MULTIPLE CONTACTS! I have two CMC cruisers in planetary orbit and one cruiser in combat position," Jess said, urgently. "We haven't been detected, yet, which is odd."

"Not really. *Stingray's* sensors can peer around objects, like planets or moons. CMC sensors are line-of-sight."

"Sensors indicate an explosion on the planet surface. Looks like two transports collided. I'm showing one hundred dead. Standby! We've been detected. One cruiser is in pursuit and will be within firing range in two minutes." The CMC cruiser detected the piece of rock as it rounded the moon, swirling out of control.

"Okay, let's get out of here. Going to full sub-light power." From the bowels of the ship came a low-pitched hum as the sub-light engines spooled up to full power.

"Eps, we haven't broken light speed yet, and the cruiser is closing."

"Wave drive is still warming up. We only have sub-light speed right now, but we should be able to maintain a slight lead."

"It's not the cruiser I'm worried about!" Jess exclaimed. "Sensors indicate a massive subterranean explosion—directly under the cabin!"

"Yeah, I rigged the chamber below the cabin to blow to destroy all traces of me being there in case I had to leave under duress. Should produce a crater and swallow the cabin."

"Um—whatever you used to blow it fractured the tectonic plate and ignited the planet's core." She pushed more buttons and sliders. "The resulting fireball just vaporized the two CMC cruisers in orbit. OH MY GOD! EPS! YOU BLEW UP THE DAMNED PLANET!"

He looked over at Jess, who had an incredulous expression on her face, and all he could think of saying was, "Oops." At that moment, the ship lurched.

"We're taking fire! Shields are holding at ninety-eight percent. We need to get out of here, Eps. There's a massive shock wave coming at us from the exploding planet." Again, the ship lurched as she took another bombardment from the CMC cruiser. "Shields are down to ninety-five percent and holding."

Opening a communication channel, Eps bellowed, "Command, CMC vessel, this is Capt. Epsilon, command *Stingray*, you need to jump to hyper-space immediately! Check your aft sensors; you're in imminent danger of being destroyed!"

"Not on your life, Epsilon!" came the heated response and another assault, rocking *Stingray*. "Your ass is mine if it's the last thing—." The COMM link went dead.

"Shields down to ninety percent and holding," Jess said. "Shockwave just vaporized the cruiser! EPS! Fifteen seconds until impact! Do something!"

A beep-beep sounded and the second of the two large sliders lit up on the console. "Engaging Wave drive, power two!" Eps slid the slider up to the "2" mark and with that space around them twisted to the right, then to the left, and then back to center. Stars shot by, all blazing in a rainbow of colors: purple, red, orange, green, blue, and white; all blurred by the incredible speed at which they were moving.

"Whew! That was close," Jess said. "Shields are at passive status."

Eps entered a course into the navigation system and *Stingray* turned to the right and slightly up. "Computer, activate normal operational protocol."

"Normal operational protocol activated. Life support

systems online," the computer confirmed.

"Let's get out of these suits," he said to Jess.

"Wave drive?" Jess asked, as they started to strip off their pressure suits. "I heard rumors about it. But I also heard that every time they tried it, it ended in some gruesome disaster."

"Well, we're alive, so I guess they must have perfected it."

"Or they stole it."

Smiling, Eps just shook his head.

"So, how does the wave drive work?"

"Well, it's the bleeding edge of technology and *Stingray* is the only ship to have it as far as I could tell. The rebellion believes the Conglomerate stole the technology, but they're not sure from whom. When you open her up full bore, she runs at over twice an order of magnitude faster than the fastest Conglomerate ship out there.

"She has tried-and-true standard sub-light engines, divided into quarter, half, and three-quarter power," Eps said, motioning to a single slider on the console. "They represent their respective sub-light fraction while full sub-light power represents just a hair under the speed of light. Kind of an oxymoron if you ask me. Engaging the wave drive provides ten power levels, one through ten, each increasing the speed of the ship according to this formula," Eps continued, as he pulled up the following formula on the screen:

$$s = p^{(\sqrt{\tan^{-1}(p)}\,)-\pi} * c$$

where
$s$=speed
$p$=power level
$c$=speed of light

"The wave drive really tops out at wave nine, a little over a half million times the speed of light. If you hit wave ten, which is a little over one million times the speed of light, theoretically a paradox would occur and you'd be catapulted into an infinite number of alternate timelines simultaneously, each one extending out from that one single point in space-time. The human brain isn't capable of existing on multiple planes at once and would explode. Have you ever seen a human brain explode? I have, and it ain't pretty."

Waving his hands as he continued, "The way the wave drive works is remarkably simple. It creates a quantum bubble of charged particles around and extending outward from the ship. It then oscillates this bubble to form a wave. Inside the bubble, the ship 'hops' forward with each oscillation. The higher the power level, the faster the bubble oscillates and the longer the wave gets, pushing the ship quicker and farther. The ship has to be equipped with primary and secondary inertial dampeners; otherwise it would be bounced around inside the bubble like a bucking bronco, only to be violently torn apart, along with her substantially more delicate crew."

Suddenly, the doors to the bridge opened. "Life support nominal," the computer announced.

"Good, the rest of the ship is now habitable. Come on, I'll give you the two-cent tour," Eps said. Timber got up and followed Eps and Jess out the door and down the metal stairs to the rear end of the second level. "Okay, starting aft is the ship's mess," Eps said, pointing in front of them as they walked through the door that opened as they approached. "The galley is off to the left. You can prepare your meals over there if you have fresh ingredients," pointing to the array of food preparation equipment. "However, as fresh ingredients are...well...scarce, we will mostly be using the food replicators. They are pre-programmed with 10 million different dishes from around the universe. The replicator will recreate whatever food item you select at the molecular level using atoms it harvests from special intake tubes on the outside of the ship. It's incredibly brilliant, but you won't see the Conglomerate promoting this device for 'humanitarian support'. Ending famine and demand for food is just not profitable. But it does make space travel a whole lot easier with less supply stops." Several tables surrounded by chairs made up the rest of the space. Large windows adorned the room, giving a stunning view of the stars shooting by.

Turning around, they headed back out into the corridor.

"First doors on the left and right are the crew's head and showers, respectively." They started walking to the forward part of the deck and Eps pointed to several doors on the right and left side of the corridor. "Crew's quarters." They stopped at two doors at the forward end of the deck. "The left door is the captain's quarters and the right door is the XO's quarters."

Pointing to the sensor next to the right door, he instructed, "Wave your hand over the sensor." She did, and the door slid open and she walked in while Eps stood in the doorway. Sitting in front of the bed were a pair of Jess's boots. On the bed were a pair of blue denim pants, a black leather jacket (both were Jess's favorites), shirt, proper undergarments, and her weapon of choice: the Kramer-2. Identical to the Kramer-1, the company added a dampener to reduce the kick. The Kramer-1 was a popular pistol, but the manufacturer gave in to the outpouring of customer comments that they should reduce the kick. "These are your quarters, Jessie. Off to the left is your private head. Get showered and changed and I'll meet you out here in a few," he said, backing out of the doorway.

Jess turned to Eps; tears welled in her eyes. "Thanks Reggie," was all she was able to get out before the door closed.

Turning to the left, he waved his hand over the sensor to his own quarters and the door slid open. It was the identical layout, just reversed and a little larger. His boots, clothes and weapons were neatly arranged in front of him. As he walked in the door, it closed behind him, but not before Timber came through and jumped up on the bed and curled up at the head of it. "Figures," he muttered. Timber ignored him as usual. Since his and Jess's quarters were at the front of the ship, the windows looked out forward and off to the side. It was an awesome sight to see the stars whiz by. He stripped off his grimy clothes and jumped into the "shower". Standing in the stall with his feet shoulder width apart and his arms extended over his head, Eps pressed the green button on the ceiling. A large circular device descended from the top; a whitish electrical looking field shimmered in the middle of it. The field enveloped Eps as it dropped down to his feet. "Ah, that was tantalizing," he exclaimed, as it passed by his man parts. It then came back up for a second pass, returning to its home in the ceiling, and Eps let out another "Ah" at the proper moment. The field was a special force field that removed dirt, dead skin cells and other foreign objects from the body. It was programmed to recognize the skin of all known species in the universe. Clean and refreshed, Eps stepped out and walked over to the sink and looked in the mirror. *Yikes!* Extracting an LPGD (laser personal grooming device), he turned it on and started dragging the beam across his face. Of course, this device is much more efficient than the old metal blade and lather, not needing shaving cream and instantly vaporizing the shaved hair. *Really miss the feel and ritual of shaving with an old-fashioned blade and hot lather.* He finished shaving and looked once again in the mirror. *Nice. Very nice.* He thought about Jess using her LPGD on her body just a mere few meters away on the other side of the wall as he turned and walked to the bed and dressed.

* * *

Sporting their fresh "uniforms", Epsilon and Jess emerged from their quarters. Eps was wearing a white shirt under a brown leather jacket and brown leather pants. "You look smart," he said to Jess, as he looked her up and down. Her hair was silky looking and tied up in her signature ponytail. He could only imagine that the rest of her was neatly groomed as well. He did good picking out her clothes. Everything fit like a glove, accenting her assets while still projecting an image of "Don't mess with me!" She was ready for business!

"Smart?" Jess asked, with a crooked smile.

"Very smart," Eps replied, looking into her eyes. He wished he could say the words he really wanted to say, but this was neither the time nor the place. He was a firm believer that there is always a time and place for everything. "Shall we continue the tour?" Turning, he headed down the metal staircase in front of them, Jess in tow. At the bottom, he faced aft and pointed to the large door in front of them and continued, "Cargo and shuttle bay, we already came from there." He turned forward and pointed to a door on the left with an access pad. "On the port side is the armory. You should already have access. Lots of neat toys in there."

He pointed to the right. Stretching along the entire right side of the corridor was a frosted glass wall with a double sliding glass door in the middle. A large caduceus was etched into the frosting of each door. "Sickbay on the starboard side. Kind of funny we still use port and starboard for spaceships, eh? In reality, all sides of the ship are 'toward the stars'." He chuckled.

"Yeah, some customs are hard to break."

"You know it really isn't glass per se. It is transparent Zillium. The whole ship is made of Zillium, the strongest and lightest metal known to man," he said, rapping his knuckles on the wall, producing a definitely metallic sound. "Blows my mind how they can make metal transparent. That's engineers for you!" Eps said, as they entered sickbay. "Private quarters and office to the left is for our yet-to-be-determined Chief Medical Officer." Along the back and side walls were counter tops with cabinets above and below. The rest of the space was broken up into four bays, separated by curtains. In each bay was a bed with display panels protruding out from the head and sides.

"State-of-the-art ship and they still have curtains separating each bed," Jess commented, shaking her head.

"Like you said, some customs are hard to break! Come on," Eps said, as they exited sickbay. "Finally, the forward door leads to the engine room." He waved his hand over the sensor, and the door opened. The two of them passed through and descended a ladder to the level below. "The private quarters and office for the Chief Engineer are straight ahead."

They turned around to face aft and were immediately drawn to the object in the center. The engine room itself was rather large and surprisingly clean and organized. The object in the center was unlike anything Jess had ever seen. It was a large shimmering purple orb, almost translucent at times, levitating between two anchoring cubes, one to the ceiling and one to the deck. Shooting out from all four corners of the top cube were two yellow and two green energy beams, all four of them connecting at the topmost point of the orb. Connecting from the bottommost point of the orb out to the four corners of the bottom cube were two blue and two red energy beams. The orb's color would darken and lighten in a rhythmic pulse that could be felt through the deck. Surrounding the orb was a light purple halo that pulsated in sync to the orb's rhythm.

"Mesmerizing, isn't it?" Eps asked.

"Yes, it is."

"If you let it, it will suck you right in—anyway, that's the Main; the heart of the wave drive."

Extending out from the bottom cube on each side was a large transparent conduit. It led off at a forty-five-degree angle and disappeared into the bulkhead on its respective sides of the compartment. "Those conduits send power to the port and starboard sub-light engines," Eps continued. "When those engines are running, you'll see red waves of energy flowing through them and the faster we go the more intense the color and flow. Likewise, with the wave drive, the faster we go, the brighter the orb's color, the faster it pulses, and the larger the halo around it gets. It is a sight to see!"

"Cool. I'll have to remember to check it out in all my spare time."

"The top cube is a positron generator. The resulting matter and antimatter are fed into the orb through the yellow and green energy beams. The orb then magically converts it into energy, which is then fed into the bottom distribution cube via the blue and red energy beams. It also creates the wave phenomenon which, of course, drives the ship.

"The wave engine is always producing energy. That's why it's tapped to also power the sub-light engines. Additionally, those smaller conduits coming out of the bottom cube that split off in multiple different directions provide power to the rest of the ship."

"Those are blue energy waves?"

"Less power than what is needed for the sub-light engines."

After a short pause, Jess asked, "So, what are we doing about essential crew?"

As if right on cue, everything around them twisted to the left, then to the right, and then back to center. "Ah, we've dropped out of wave, we must have arrived. Come on!" Eps said excitedly, as he headed up to the bridge.

* * *

Eps and Jess assumed the same stations after they entered the bridge. Jess noticed the main screen was outlined in a red stripe. Looking at her console, she exclaimed, "WHOA! We're cloaked. We have cloaking ability?"

"Yup. I programmed her to automatically cloak when we drop out of wave. More of a convenience as I expected to be a one man show flying her." Showing on the screen was a blue planet. "Assuming standard orbit; welcome to Kempledore, home to my good friend Taliriktug. It's a pretty primitive, out of the way planet, so there shouldn't be any orbital traffic. The AutoNav will keep her a respectable distance from any ship that ventures too close."

At the mention of Taliriktug, Timber sauntered onto the bridge, whining. "I know, fella. Come on. Let's go see him," Eps replied to Timber, scratching him behind his ears.

As the three of them headed down to the transport platform, Eps continued, "Taliriktug has Timber's mother and father. He gave me Timber when I went into hiding. It will be safest for him to go back to his family now. Plus, I have a few things I need to pick up. Taliriktug also has an ear to the ground and will know where we can find Crash." Jimmy "Crash" Zubreé was a very talented ex-Alliance pilot who served under Epsilon aboard the *Freedom*. Eps never met a more capable pilot.

"Crash went into hiding," Jess said. "He did some flying for the resistance, driving blockade runners. The Conglomerate has a price on his head. I don't know how open he will be."

"They have a price on our heads, too."

"Touché."

They arrived at the transport platform and as Jess stepped on, Eps entered in the coordinates and stepped on himself. Facing Jess, he wrapped his arms around her and positioned Timber in between their legs.

"Um—something you want to tell me, Eps?" she asked.

"We're transporting into a tight space; a closet, to be precise. Need to make sure he hasn't been compromised." He pushed a button on his communicator/sensor device and they dematerialized on *Stingray* and re-materialized in a utility closet on the planet.

"UGH!" Jess croaked, as she fought to keep her balance. Eps tightened his grip around her to help steady her.

"Not to worry, you'll get used to it," Eps whispered, as he reluctantly unwrapped his arms from around Jess. Cracking the door open, he peered out. Seeing it was clear, he opened it the rest of the way and cautiously started out into a hallway. All of a sudden, he was knocked aside as Timber almost bowled him over, lurching out of the closet and bounding down the hall.

"Timber, ol' boy! It's good to see you!" a deep voice bellowed from a room at the end of the hallway. Two other similar looking Husky/Malamute dogs appeared at the end of the hall, growling. Jess instinctively put her hand on her gun as they walked toward the dogs. Coming around the corner behind the dogs was a towering one-armed man. "Reginald my old friend! Good to see you are still alive and kicking!"

"Aye, it is good to see you," Eps replied, cracking a wide smile as the two men embraced. All three dogs turned around and went back into the room and curled up by the fire. "Jess, this is my friend Taliriktug. Tal, this is my friend and former XO, Jessie Smythe."

"Hi. Nice to meet you," Jess said, extending the hand that had earlier been gripping her gun. Taking her hand, Tal kissed the top of it.

"AHA! It is a distinct honor and privilege to finally meet the much talked about Lt. Jessie Smythe!" Tal said. "Epsilon, you ol' dog, you. You said she was perfect; but she's more than perfect. She's extraordinarily beautiful and captivatingly sexy! You been holding out on me?"

Jess smirked and turned a shade of crimson. "Perfect?" she asked, giving Eps a wry look.

"Tal, you know that's not appropriate!" Eps admonished.

"You bet your skinny little ass that's not appropriate!" an Amazon looking woman who appeared behind Tal said.

"Lena! You still putting up with 'His Crankiness'?" Eps asked, pointing his thumb at Tal and cracking another wide smile. Lena was as tall as Tal and just as fierce looking. She had long blond hair and blue eyes. Her body was tightly toned, and she was wearing very short black leather shorts and a lace up front leather bustier that couldn't quite manage to hold all of her womanhood in. They'd been married ever since he met the two of them a decade ago. Lena gave Eps a bear hug, lifting him a good foot and half off the ground, much to Jess's amusement. After plopping him back down, he continued, "Lena, this is Jess. Jess, this is Lena, Tal's wife."

"Hi," Jess said, shaking hands with Lena.

"Pleasure's mine."

"Listen, Tal, we're under a time crunch," Eps started.

"When aren't you under a time crunch?" Tal roared, laughingly. "What do you need?"

"First, I need to leave Timber with you. Second, I need my footlocker I entrusted to you. And lastly, I need to know where Crash is."

"Still very needy, I see, Reginald," Lena said, in a mocking tone. "You're not going anywhere until after dinner. Come, the meal is almost ready. Sit down and have a drink."

Eps and Tal looked at each other and shrugged. They knew it was futile to argue with her. So, Eps, Tal and Jess obeyed and took seats around the table. Lena poured glasses of red wine for everyone.

"I can't believe how they made you out to be such a horrible criminal, Eps," Lena said. "All of those lies about you being a terrorist; killing children. We didn't kill anyone; we made sure everyone was off the station before destroying it."

"Well," Eps said. "I have big shoulders. I can take it if it keeps it off other people."

"Um—wait a minute," Jess interrupted. "What is this 'we' business?" Lena got quiet; the color drained from her face as she realized she may have just slipped up. She looked at Eps with a horrified look.

"Ha, ha," Tal roared, amused at his wife's discomfort. "What, my dear Jess, you think 'Mr. Larger-Than-Life' here did all that by himself?" Tal roared again in laughter. Eps just shook his head.

"Oh, pray tell," Jess laughed. "I want to hear all about this!"

"Well, after Eps went AWOL, he came to me with this crazy-assed plan to steal *Stingray* and destroy all the data and research about her...."

* * *

Eps, Tal, and Lena were crammed inside a crate in the cargo hold of a private supply ship en route to Research Station Nox. Since the Conglomerate was made up of companies, it stood to reason that they would contract out services. One of those services was to ferry supplies to Conglomerate outposts. For security reasons, they liked to use owner-operators for the sensitive jobs; they felt it was easier, more cost efficient, and resulted in tighter security only having to perform detailed background checks on a single person versus an entire company. The company that had the contract for Research Station Nox was Bubba's Hauling, owned by Bubba, of course. While Bubba knew the ins and outs of hauling and always met his delivery schedules, Bubba appeared to be dumber than a box of rocks. If you tried to engage him in conversation, all you would get back is a blank stare, unless, of course, you talked about hauling. He was the joke of the hauling industry, so when he came up for security review, the examiners may not have given him as thorough a background check as they should have.

What they didn't know was that Bubba's real name was Bob Hill, a retired Special Forces sergeant from the Earth's Marine Corps and a member of the resistance. Tal knew this. Having sold one of his dogs to him a few years prior, he hooked Bubba up with the resistance, even though Tal wasn't actively involved in it. So, when Eps approached Tal with the plan of stealing *Stingray*, Tal knew exactly who to go to.

Eps could tell the ship was slowing and shortly after that he could feel the ship bump up against the docking bay. *Amateurs!* They had arrived, finally. Two sharp raps on the crate brought him out of his trance; it was a tight squeeze getting the three of them into this crate and he wanted out badly.

"Heads up," Bubba whispered, in a thick Louisiana accent. "It's show time."

Eps rapped the crate wall twice in acknowledgement. He could hear the cargo doors open and crates starting to be unloaded.

"Hey Bubba, how's it shaking?" somebody laughed. Eps assumed it was one of the station's guards.

"Ran inna some unusual asteroid activity yestadaay," Bubba answered. "Dat crate over dere," he pointed to the one that Eps, Tal, and Lena were in. "Isa special delivery from," he looked at his paper manifest, "Special Projects Section to sumtin' called 'Project *Stingray*'." Using a paper manifest, instead of a computerized manifest, gave more credence to Bubba's cover of being too stupid to use a computer.

"We'll have to inspect it. Open it up."

"Naw, sir! Itsa sealed 'Top Secret'. I ain't openin' it on me boat. You guys unload it and then if you wanna to break da seal, thatta yo bidness. Bubba has no part o'dat bidness. YOU go to jail for breakin' top secret seal; not Bubba!"

"Fine," the guard motioned to workers to come over. "Take this directly to Section 3."

* * *

The crate was delivered to the hangar bay that contained *Stingray*, identified as 'Section 3.' Nobody stopped it, scanned it, or questioned it. Nobody wanted to be the one to be interrogated for sticking their nose into a top-secret operation. Had they opened or scanned the crate, they would have seen it chock full of odd-looking components, courtesy of a 3D holographic generator inside the crate.

Timing was everything. The crate arrived just as the workers were clearing for the day, so no one saw the three emerge from the crate. Looking around, Eps quickly got his bearings. "Lena, stand guard at the door."

"Got it," she said, and positioned herself at the door looking out.

"Tal, there's a terminal over there to upload the virus. I hope the login codes you got are accurate."

"It will work," Tal responded. "My source is solid."

"Right. I'm heading to the bridge." Eps climbed up a ladder and disappeared into the cargo hold of *Stingray*.

* * *

Tal was busy whacking away at the terminal's keyboard with his one good hand. "Here goes nothing," he said, after entering in the credentials and hitting the login key. The command cursor presented itself on the screen. He let out a sigh, realizing that he had been holding his breath. Deep down he thought the alarms would go off and marines would storm in and grab them. He removed the crystal that his source provided him with from his pocket and inserted it into the terminal's port. He then typed in the command to initiate the virus. The login that was provided had sufficient clearance to allow the program on the crystal to pass through the firewall and override the virus protection. The virus was designed to specifically target any information that was tied to or referenced *Project Stingray* and overwrite it with smiley faces. That was Lena's idea; normally to securely wipe data the program overwrites it with ones and zeros, but it really doesn't matter what characters are used. The program spawned a second and third program. The second one jumped out onto the network, looking for all the backup systems. Its mission was to tell each of the backup systems to immediately perform a security format on each and every backup crystal in each and every backup library throughout the Conglomerate's network. In the name of corporate efficiency, the backup crystals were housed in a very large vault and were never removed off site. The vault was believed to be indestructible. The third program also jumped out onto the network and infiltrated each and every device on the network. Its job was to detect the presence of and/or reference to *Project Stingray* and securely delete it. Programs one and two also found the pipe that led out to the Conglomerate's main network that connected to every single device in existence. While they had their work cut out for them, the programs would patiently hop from device to device and perform their tasks. Within six hours of loading the virus, all the backups within the Conglomerate network had been silently formatted and wouldn't be noticed until someone needed something restored. Over the next seventy-two hours, all references to *Project Stingray* were secretly destroyed before system administrators noticed something awry. Their first, and only, line of defense would be to restore from backups. A lot of guts would come to be wrenched when these folks realized that their primary, secondary, and tertiary backup systems were gone. Totally and utterly gone.

* * *

"Security patrol coming," Lena loudly whispered to Tal from the door.

"Come on," Tal said, grabbing the crystal out of the terminal. They headed behind the crate as they wouldn't make it to the ladder without being seen. The door to the corridor opened and two guards entered and were in a heated debate about the game last night and only performed a cursory check. After all, how could anyone penetrate their tight perimeter security? One of them, however, noticed the terminal that Tal had been using was still logged in.

"Hey, check this out. One of the brilliant minds

left their terminal logged in," one of the guards said.

"Great," the other guard replied. "Now we're gonna be stuck here for hours waiting for the moron to come back here and log off the terminal."

"Yeah, but we'll get over-time! I'll call it in," the first guard said, as he pulled out his communicator.

"Gentlemen," Tal said, popping out from behind the crate and leveling a Kramer-1 at them. "I wouldn't do that if I were you." Without further fanfare, he shot them both.

"I hope you set it on stun," Lena said, joining her husband. "Otherwise, Eps is going to have a bird."

"Of course, I don't want to kill anybody!" They dragged the unconscious bodies out of the direct line-of-sight of the door.

* * *

Eps too had a crystal provided by Tal's source. He arrived on the bridge and quickly found the port on one of the consoles and inserted the crystal. He entered in the provided credentials and it too produced a command prompt. He then entered in the proper command and waited. Nothing happened. Tal and Lena appeared on the bridge.

"Virus launched Eps," Tal said. "We ran into a security patrol and had to neutralize them." Eps whipped around and looked at his friend. "Relax, I only stunned them." Eps relaxed and turned back to the console.

"How are we doing here?" Lena asked.

"I don't know," Eps worried. "I did as instructed, but nothing happened."

"He said to be patient," Tal replied.

Suddenly, all the lights in the hangar went out. A few seconds later emergency lighting came on, the station's klaxon sounded, emitting the shrill low-to-high pitched sound and the station-wide COMM bellowed: "Emergency condition alert! All personnel proceed to evacuation shuttles immediately! All personnel abandon station! All personnel abandon station! Core meltdown in five minutes."

The three of them looked at each other, bewildered. The terminal beeped and displayed:

```
Ready to depart
```

The program closed and secured the airlock doors in the cargo bay, raised the shields, and powered up the maneuvering thrusters. It then released the docking clamps with a loud BOOM, rocking *Stingray*. She swayed a bit, her port wing bumping some equipment, causing it to burst into flames as it touched the shields. Eps gained control of *Stingray* and swiveled her around to the bay door. In all the commotion, they didn't notice that the program had opened the door to space.

"Okay, let's get out of here!" Eps said.

"You know how to fly this thing?" Tal asked.

"We'll find out real soon," Eps smiled.

"There's a force field blocking the opening," Lena said.

"Not to worry," Eps replied. "It's low level, to keep atmospheric containment in the bay. We can pass through it."

Suddenly the shields pulsed bright several times. "We're taking fire," Tal said.

"No worries," Eps replied, calmly. "The guards must have regained consciousness. Their small-

arms fire is no match for *Stingray*'s shields." Eps
guided the ship out of the hangar and into space.
Once she cleared the station, Eps engaged the cloak
and made a wide loop and came to a stop. It took
about 15 minutes to totally evacuate the station.
"According to the sensors, there's nobody left on
the station. Time to blow it." Eps turned to the
terminal; it displayed:

`Destroy?`

He typed in:

`Yes`

The station exploded.

* * *

"So, see Jess, there wasn't anybody left on the station,"
Lena said.
"I knew Eps would never kill anybody that he didn't need
to," Jess replied.
They finished eating and reminisced about the good old
days. Jess just listened and absorbed it all in, stealing long glances
at Eps.
Lena leaned over and whispered into Eps's ear, "You two
make such a nice-looking couple."
Eps just closed his eyes and shook his head.
"You best listen to her," Tal laughed. "Whatever she said!"

* * *

Eps and Jess re-materialized back on *Stingray*. "That's the
best meal I've had in a long, long time," Jess said.
"Lena is a damned fine cook. She can make a tasty meal

out of just about anything," Eps responded. They were carrying the heavy footlocker across the cargo bay.

"So, what did she whisper in your ear?" Jess asked, with a "come hither" smile.

"Sweet nothings!" Eps replied, coyly. He waved his hand over a panel on the wall, and a tray extended from it. They hoisted the footlocker up and into the tray and let it down with a thud. Eps touched the panel, and it retracted back into the wall. "Yeah, perfect hiding places," Eps answered Jess's silent question, motioning around the cargo bay. There were hundreds of these identical panels all around the bay. Even if one looked closely, finding the ones that stored secret cargo would literally be like trying to find a needle in a haystack.

They headed up to the bridge where they assumed their positions. Eps broke orbit, moving the left slider to the ¾ position and guided the ship away from Kempledore. "Setting three-quarter sub-light power. It's not a good idea to engage the wave drive while in the gravitational field of a planet. Bad things can happen."

*Stingray* pulled away from the planet quickly and Eps entered the coordinates that Tal gave him into the NAV system. "Going to Wave power four," he said, as he slid the right slider to the "4" mark. Again, everything around them twisted to the right, then to the left, and then back to the center. "We should be at Nubia in about 24 hours. You take first watch. I'll relieve you in 10 hours."

"Aye, Captain," she said, settling into the command chair.

Eps raised an eyebrow at that move but didn't say anything as he left the bridge. The doors opened as he approached and closed behind him. Entering his quarters, he stripped down to his trunks, splashed some cool water over his face, and plopped down on the bed. As he lay there, he realized that he already missed Timber. *Did Timber miss me?* That was the last thought he had before he fell fast asleep.

Jess got up from the command chair, looked nervously at the door and sat down in the right seat. Pressing buttons, she established an audio-only communication channel.

"Yes?" barked a male voice over the COMM.

"You were right. He has *Stingray*," she said.

After a short pause, "Where is he taking her?"

"I don't know. He's assembling a crew. I want to talk to Maggie."

"You're not in a position to demand anything," the man bellowed. "You deliver *Stingray*, I deliver Maggie. Is that clear?"

"Crystal."

"I want to know what he is doing and where he is going. I want *Stingray* back."

"I've never been in this sector before. We are too far away from any CMC assets and I don't even think we are in Conglomerate space. I have to go and will report back the next chance I can steal away." She terminated the COMM link and buried her head in her hands. She started to cry. "What did I get you into, Maggie? I'm so sorry. God Eps, I need you more than ever." Her voice trailed off into sobs.

## CHAPTER THREE

Eps and Jess were only on planet for five minutes and Eps had this nagging feeling that they were being watched.

"You're just paranoid, Eps," Jess responded to his silent question.

"Maybe; maybe not," Eps said.

They parked *Stingray* on the far side of Nubia's first moon, hidden in a canyon and cloaked for good measure. Using one of the shuttles, they landed on the planet undetected as the shuttle also had cloaking ability. Nubia is a beautiful planet; her inhabitants vary greatly by species. The "people" of Nubia just want to live in a peaceful setting and are very friendly. Any Nubian would offer a stranger shelter and a meal if asked. They were not pleased with the extra security forces "provided" by the Conglomerate Military Command.

"There's the bar," Jess said, pointing to a building off to the left. "Tal said Crash frequented this particular bar."

It reminded Eps of a saloon during the "Wild West" period on Earth. As they approached the entrance, a sign read "No Weapons Allowed".

"Yeah, like that's gonna happen," Epsilon quipped. Both he and Jess were wearing leather jackets with special carry holsters built in, concealing a Kramer-2 sub-compact laser pistol. The holsters were lined with a special thread, spun by Lipitus spiders. The thread absorbs energy, rendering the contents of the holster practically invisible to scanners. Adding to that, the Kramer-2 was constructed with materials designed to evade detection by scanners. This prompted the Conglomerate to outlaw its sale, purchase, and ownership except, of course, to the Conglomerate military. Even though it was small in stature, fitting in the palm of your hand, the Kramer-2 could down a raging Pungdon Bull in full heat.

"Arms out," ordered the huge bouncer at the door. Both Eps and Jess complied, and he ran the scanner up and down their bodies. He gave Jess a thorough up and down with his eyes, pausing the scanner at all her "right places". Jess just looked at him and smiled that "I'll twist your head off and spit down your spine" smile. "Go on in and have a nice day," he told the pair, watching her backside as she walked by.

They entered the bar, and it was pretty crowded. The throng of different looking beings all eating and drinking together immediately brought back memories of pre-Conglomerate days. Eps had encountered most of these races on his many travels throughout the universe.

"Hey there, big boy," a scantily clad, purple-skinned female with three breasts said, while running her finger across Eps's chest. This brought him out of his reminiscent trance.

"Hey, slut, he's with me!" Jess admonished the intruder. The tramp just laughed and kept walking, seeking out another man.

A big u-shaped bar stood in the middle of the room. Several rows of tables and chairs flanked the bar outward. Finally, along the walls were booths. The pair walked up to an empty spot at the bar.

"Ah, greetings," the bartender said, as he started mixing a drink. "I think a classic Earth drink for the gorgeous lady Jess: a Long Island Iced Tea," he continued, smiling at Jess while handing her the glass. "I apologize for using Nubian lemon, but authentic Earth lemon is very, very hard to come by these days." Jess had an amazed look on her face, not believing he knew who she was. "And for the good Captain Epsilon, his once in a great while drink: A Solar Flare with a twist of Nubian Lime and mixed, authentically I might add, with a Sticky Finger and not a swizzle stick," the bartender continued, as he mixed up the concoction in a large glass, utilizing many different liquors and a Sticky Finger.

"Do I know you?" Epsilon asked.

"Here you go," the bartender said, as he handed over the glass to Eps.

"A Solar Flare?" Jess queried. "And how did you know what his favorite is? And how do you know who I am? Or what drink I would like?" Now she too was becoming a little nervous that their clandestine visit to Nubia to find Crash may not be as clandestine as she had hoped.

"So many questions, this one, and so little time. He never told you the story of the Solar Flare? There are only three beings in the entire universe that can handle more than one Solar Flare! Maybe four if you count the King," he said, shaking his head from side-to-side. "But personally, I don't think he counts."

"No," she answered, looking back and forth between the bartender and Eps, and showing a mark of inquisitiveness.

"Seriously, do I know you?" Eps asked, again.

Ignoring him, the bartender continued. "My! My! Legend has it, and feel free to jump in at any time," he started, first looking at Jess, then to Eps, and back to Jess. "On the planet Daehkarf, in the Pewbeez sector, there were these two individuals: Mr. Postmodernist and the outstandingly hot Mira that concocted this drink one night out of sheer boredom and, after many tastes, named it a Solar Flare with a twist of Nubian Lime. Now, you may ask, what's a Sticky Finger? Well, in the absence of any swizzle sticks, our brew masters used, well, a sticky finger, adding a unique flavor to this unique libation. There is no mention of what exactly a Sticky Finger is, but I can get authentic replicas of them from a very reclusive supplier on Daehkarf," he said, with a raspy laugh and a wink at Jess. "Anyway, our good Captain here ran into these two fine folk on a visit to that odd planet and they boasted that there wasn't anyone in the universe that could handle their concoction. To our good Captain here, those were fightin' words. So, a few Solar Flares later, the trio, not of their right minds, decided to storm the castle. Now, the reigning king at the time, a handsome man by the name of Moctezuma Straycat (lovingly referred to as 'King Mocty' by his loyal subjects) would not be out drunk by these scowls. To make a long story even longer, there was enough swill left for another two rounds. Suffice it to say, when morning came, Her Royal Hotness, Queen Zorya, found King Mocty passed out, completely naked, and sprawled half on and half off the royal 'throne'," the bartender used his fingers to simulate quote signs around the word throne and gave a hissing laugh. "The trio was nowhere to be found with Mr. Postmodernist and Mira denying the whole affair ever happened, as they probably truly didn't have any recollection of that entire night. It is said that King Mocty was never quite the same after that fateful night...," he finished, his voice trailing off.

"OKAY, this is getting old. Who are you?" Epsilon demanded.

Moving a little closer to the two of them, looking around nervously, and lowering his voice, he continued in a covert tone. "In the very near future, my dear Captain, certain actions may not be what they really seem. Remember that." This caused both Jess and Epsilon to wrinkle their brows, trying to figure out what he meant. "And—he who you are looking for is in the corner booth over there," he said, motioning to the back corner of the barroom over his shoulder with his head. Eps noticed a rather large black guy slip out the back door near the booth the bartender motioned to. Straightening up and resuming normal conversational tone the bartender laughed, "And OF COURSE, Captain, you know who I am! My name is Gary Zeiger." With that, he turned on his heels and headed down to the end of the bar and disappeared.

"Wow, that was, well, strange," Jess said. "So, is all that true? How do you know him?"

Ignoring her, Eps said, "Come on, there's Crash in the corner," and he started off toward the booth. Jess shrugged her shoulders, knowing Eps wasn't going to expound, and followed him.

Eps and Jess walked up to the booth occupied by Crash and

another man. "Hey Crash, long time no see!" Eps said. Crash turned toward him, smiled that broad toothy smile that caused the ladies to swoon and stood up. Crash had a skinny, but not scrawny, build, well-tanned skin, slicked back black hair, and blue eyes. He reminded Eps of an Italian Mafioso who would sooner drop you as much as look at you. That was the outside. Inside, he had a heart of gold and would give you the shirt off his back if you needed it.

"Epsilon!" Crash exclaimed, vigorously shaking his hand. "Jess!" he continued, giving her a big hug. "It's great to see you. Rumor had it you both were dead."

"Obviously, Jimmy, the rumor is wrong," Jess countered, motioning to herself with her hands.

"Join us," Crash said, motioning to the seats. Jess sat next to Jimmy and Eps sat down next to the other guy, looking him up and down. "This is my good friend Max, the best engineer I've ever met. There isn't an engine or system he can't keep running! Max, this is Captain Epsilon. He was my captain on the *Freedom*."

Max was a short, stocky fellow with light brown, unkempt hair, and brown eyes. His fair complexion was the result of spending most of his time in an engine room. Eps noted an oddness about him but couldn't really put his finger on it. Maybe a cross between a younger version of Doc Brown from the old earth film *Back to the Future* and Kramer from the old earth show *Seinfeld*, two shows he recently saw on the Mega Oldies channel on VidiNet.

"Pleasure to meet the infamous Captain Epsilon," Max said, shaking hands.

"Pleasure's mine," Eps retorted. "Max, what?"

"I don't know. Everyone's just called me 'Max'."

"Hmm."

"And this is Lt. Jessie Smythe. She was my XO aboard the *Freedom*," Crash continued.

"It is DEFINITELY my pleasure to meet you, my dear," crooned Max, taking Jess's hand and lightly kissing the top of it.

"It's nice to meet you too," Jess giggled.

"So, what brings you to this neck of the woods?" Crash

asked Eps.

"I'm putting together a crew for a rescue mission. If you're not too busy, I sure could use you."

"Who are we rescuing?"

"Maggie," Jess interjected.

Crash turned to Jess with an incredulous look. "Your sister Maggie?"

"Yeah," Jess solemnly returned. "Admiral Roth has her at Prison-12."

Max let out a low whistle.

"Count me in," Crash said, without hesitation. "But on one condition." All heads turned toward Crash. He pulled out what looked like a small piece of clear, flexible plastic. Tapping it, an image of a striking red headed woman appeared. "This is Tamson Alexandria. She's my baby sister. She's the smartest, youngest doctor around and was the personal physician to Zane White."

"Zane White, the late president and CEO of Appmicro Corporation?" Jess asked.

"Yes. To make a long story short, he had an incurable disease. Tamson did everything she could to make his remaining time bearable. Even kept him alive well past the point where other doctors said he should have died. Zane appreciated her immensely. His son, Todd, however, didn't have the same feelings after she turned down his numerous advances. After the old man died, Todd took over Appmicro and his father's seat on the Conglomerate board of directors. He made one final pitch to Tamson to marry him. When she refused, it was easy for him to use his new power and influence to have her arrested on some trumped-up charges of negligence in the death of his father. He wanted her sent to Prison-12 just for spite. The other board members, not wanting the attention that would bring, secretly nixed that order and had her put in the Women's Correctional Facility on Taurus-9. I figured out a way to get her out, but, well, I don't have the firepower or talent I need. Until now, that is."

Eps and Jess looked at each other.

"Fine," Eps said. "We'll break her out after we get Maggie.

Lord knows we can't get in anymore trouble after that job."

"No," Crash stated firmly, a little waver in his voice. "We break her out first. Besides, we are going to need a doctor on the mission, anyway."

Eps started to object, but Jess cut him off. "He's right. We are going to need a top-notch doctor. Rumblings I heard throughout the CMC before I was made Roth's personal whipping girl was that she's the best. A lot of officers were upset at her imprisonment. A couple of them resigned in protest because they had family members who were saved by her."

Crash knew Eps would take Jess's endorsement of this side mission. "So, what am I driving?"

"A ship," Eps retorted, a little irritation in his voice at being overridden by his XO. He knew, in reality, this was Jess's operation. He was just along as the adult supervision. If she was okay with this delay, then he was fine with it. Besides, it would give them an "easy" practice rescue to work out the kinks of working together. The Women's Correctional Facility on Taurus-9 was a low security facility, protected only by an outdated force field. He was confident that between Crash and Max, they would find and exploit its weakness.

"Well, DUH!" Crash quipped, but quickly lowered his head and softened his tone. "Sorry, Captain, no disrespect intended."

"I'll surprise you."

"You have *Stingray*, don't you?" Max interjected excitedly.

Eps gave him a long, hard, mildly annoyed look.

"He's cool," Crashed stated. "I trust Max with my life." He lowered his voice and continued. "We served together in the resistance."

"Well, then," Eps started slowly, still staring at Max. Normally, when you are on the receiving end of those piercing eyes, it makes you rather uncomfortable. Max wasn't fazed at all; he just sat there staring right back. "If Crash says you're 'okay', then you're okay in my book. Are you as good as he says you are?"

"Oh, I'm good all right!" Max boasted in a wide-eyed,

peculiar sort of way.

"Right. So, I suppose you want in on this little exercise too?" Eps asked him.

"Hell, freakin' yeah!" Max exclaimed, still wide-eyed. "Especially if *Stingray* is involved." He was salivating at the chance to engineer on the state-of-the-art warship that had been propelled to legendary status.

"Good," Eps said, looking around the table. "Let's get going then. Time's a wastin'."

* * *

The four of them left the bar and headed back toward the hidden shuttle. As they crossed a deserted open square, Eps and Jess gave each other a nervous look. Something was wrong. Before either of them could put their hands inside their jackets to retrieve their weapons, half a dozen Conglomerate security officers spilled out of a doorway, pointing rifles at them.

"HALT!" one of them yelled.

"What can we do for you, officer?" Crash asked, flashing that disarming smile of his.

"SHUT UP! We've been watching you. Figured it was only a matter of time before these two fugitives showed up," the officer said, motioning to Eps and Jess with his rifle. "We intend to take the lot of you in and collect the bounty on your heads and will shoot any of you if you so much as move a muscle the wrong way. You're wanted dead or alive. Makes no difference to me."

"We're worth more alive, though," Eps retorted.

"Yeah, but while dead is less credits, it's also less risk."

"True," Eps said, matter-of-factly. "Just one minor problem, though: as Conglomerate security officers, you aren't eligible for a bounty. It's your duty to bring us in."

The officer laughed. "We've enlisted the aid of a blacky stooge. He'll collect the bounty, bring it to us, we kill him, split the bounty and no one's the wiser! NOW MOVE!" He ushered them toward the door he came out of. "Any funny business and we'll shoot you dead right where you stand!" As they approached the door, it opened, and a large black man emerged; the same large black guy Eps saw slip out the back door of the bar earlier. He was tall, bald, and solidly built. He wore a black vest that didn't quite close in the front and black pants. Eps could see the fierce bravado on the top but was willing to bet deeper down there was a gentleness in there; a gentle giant.

"Bear?" Crash exclaimed.

Max got all riled up; turning sixteen shades of purple, to the point Eps grabbed him by his shirt collar to keep him from charging the officers. "You traitor, you. I hope you rot in hell for all eternity!"

Eps recalled the bartender's words: *In the very near future, certain actions may not be what they really seem. Remember that.* He detected Bear give the slightest smirk and wink at Crash. "We have a problem," Bear said. The lead officer turned in time to see Bear toss a canister on the ground toward the group of officers. The canister made a soft "pop" sound and the two officers closest to Bear crumpled to the ground as the shock wave took them out. Eps seized the opportunity to jump the first officer and wrestled him to the ground, snapping his neck with a loud, gut-wrenching crack in the process. At the same time, Max, who was already spun up, pile-drove the fourth officer, wrestled his rifle and, straining, turned it around and fired, vaporizing a hole in the officer's chest large enough to put his arm through.

The remaining two officers were too far away for Jess or Crash to tackle as the officers ran and took cover behind a wall. Jess and Crash dropped to the ground in time to evade the laser bolts coming from the officers behind the wall. Jess had her weapon out returning fire. The three of them were pinned down, out in the open.

"Fall back to the drainage ditch," Eps yelled. "I have you covered." He opened fire on the officers' position as the three others retreated and joined him in the ditch.

"We can't let them call this in," Jess said.

"I know." Eps saw the door to the building open a little and

Bear emerged, pistol in hand. The two remaining officers popped up and started firing wildly toward the four of them, forcing them to take cover. Suddenly the firing stopped. As fast as it started, it was over.

"All clear," Bear bellowed.

Eps looked at Jess, "On three." Jess nodded. "One, two, three." They both popped up over the top, weapons trained. They didn't make it too far before they saw the two officers slumped over the wall, dead. Bear was lowering his pistol, having just shot them.

Jess covered the open ground quickly and pointed her pistol at Bear. "DROP IT!"

"Hey, I had your back!"

"I—SAID—DROP—IT—NOW!

"Bear, do as she says," Crash said, as the three of them caught up to her. "She's libel to shoot you out of spite." Reluctantly, Bear laid down the weapon, growling the whole time. "Eps, we heard rumors that someone was close to tracking us down. We didn't know who. When you showed up at the bar, I breathed a sigh of relief, figuring it was you who was looking for us the whole time. Bear was tracking down a lead when you arrived. Obviously, you weren't the only ones looking for us."

"I overheard these two talking about you coming here," Bear said, pointing to the lead officer and another nearby. "I knew that you and Crash were tight, so I piped up that I knew Crash and could tip these guys off when you showed up. I saw you at the bar and slipped out the back door. I figured, using you, we could turn the tables and get the heat off all of us. Buy us some time to slip off planet and relocate."

"Crash?" Eps asked.

"The three of us have been lying low after our ship went down when we ran into a Conglomerate cruiser. We escaped, but the remaining survivors weren't so lucky; they were executed right then and there after being tortured for information. They never gave it up. The Conglomerate would love to get their hands on us and glean whatever intel they can from us on the resistance.

Which, by the way, is next to nothing."

"My plan all along was to eliminate whoever was after us," Bear said.

Eps looked around. The area was deserted, except for a young Nubian couple that watched the entire encounter, stark terror on their faces. Eps walked over to them, the male instinctively protecting his mate.

"'Bout time someone stood up to them," the Nubian said, a slight quiver in his voice.

"Had to be done," Eps replied.

"We didn't see anything."

"Good. Now get out of here before a patrol comes looking for them."

The two Nubians took off running. Eps returned to the group and met Crash's eyes, and they exchanged a silent dialog. He looked to Jess, who still had her weapon trained on Bear. He gave a good long look at Bear. "Stand down, Lieutenant. We need to hide these bodies and get out of here tout 'de suite."

Jess holstered her weapon, picked up Bear's pistol, and shoved the barrel of it in his gut as he was taking it from her. "If you compromise this mission, I will personally kill you in the most painful and hideous way possible," she stated calmly. Bear took the pistol from her and holstered it, emitting a low growl. But he believed her.

"He's good, Jess," Crash told her. She gave him a slight nod, showing no emotion in her face.

"Bear, what?" Eps asked Bear.

He chuckled. "It's just a nick name. Tobias Dickee at your service, sir," Bear said, extending his hand. Eps took it and returned the shake. He extended it to Jess, who did likewise.

"Right. Bear it is then," Eps said. "What was that canister you tossed?"

"I call it a stunner. Unfortunately, I haven't perfected it yet. It kinda backfired."

"Looked like it took down a couple combatants to me." Crash observed.

"Yeah, but it should have taken them all out," Bear continued. "Something malfunctioned. I'll have to look into it some more. I need to retrieve some supplies before we leave," Bear continued.

"I'll go with him," Max said. "Where should we meet back up?"

"Negative," Eps commanded. "Max, Crash, you're with me. We need to dispose of the bodies."

"That building we came out of is empty and abandoned," Bear offered.

"Jess, you're with Bear," Eps continued. "Rendezvous back at the shuttle."

"Aye, sir," Jess turned to Bear. "Move out."

"Jess, there's a green duffel bag. Will you grab it, please?" Crash asked.

"Sure." Jess and Bear disappeared around a corner.

The three guys started dragging the bodies of the officers into the building.

"It's great to be back together again, Captain," Crash said, with genuine happiness in his voice.

"Yes, it is, Jimmy. Yes, it is," Eps agreed.

* * *

Their return to *Stingray* was uneventful, none the wiser that the five of them had come and gone. The shuttle settled into her spot in the cargo bay, and the door opened. Her engines hadn't even had time to spool down before Max bounded out the door. He was looking wildly looking around, going from console to transporter pad. "Holy cow, transporter technology," he spurted out. "Oh my god! Where's the engine room? I have to see her power plant!"

"All in good time, Max," Eps said, as he exited the shuttle, chuckling to himself. "Max, have you ever served in the military?"

"No. The Conglomerate raided our town, looking for resistance fighters. There weren't any there, but they insisted there were. Killed a few townsfolk before they were convinced we weren't hiding anyone. Typical idiots that they were, they had the wrong town. Two towns over, the resistance had a Conglomerate Striker ship that they couldn't get to work. I decided at that moment, I would give my technical assistance to the resistance and marched right over and knocked on their door. The rest, as they say, is history."

"Bear, how about you?"

"Naw, I just bounced around from job to job. Whoever needed some muscle, I was your guy. Gave me the ability to do what I really liked doing," Bear answered.

"Oh? And what was that?"

"Inventing stuff to help soldiers," he said, grabbing one of the bags off the floor and pulling out what looked like an oversized grenade. "Like this."

"Whoa!" Jess yelled, reaching for her gun.

"No, no, it's not what you think. This is really cool. Say there's a breach in a wall or bulkhead. You pull the pin, toss it in the hole, and it 'explodes' to create a strong patch," Bear said, beaming.

"Just put it back," Jess said, relaxing. Bear put the device back in his bag.

"Very cool," Eps said. "Right, then. Lieutenant, please assign quarters to the crew and stow Bear's toys in the armory. I'll lay in a course for Taurus-9. Everyone get settled and meet in the mess in an hour. Crash, you're with me. Dismissed."

"Aye, Captain. Bear grab your crap. This way everyone," barked Lieutenant Smythe.

## CHAPTER FOUR

Captain Epsilon was showing Crash the flight deck and controls while laying in a course for Taurus-9.

"Wow, this is one helluva ride, Captain!" Crash said, excitedly.

"Yeah, she can definitely get out of her own way and then some. Think you can handle her?" Eps asked.

"Absolutely. You won't be disappointed."

"You've never disappointed me yet. Just try not to crash into anything, Crash!" Eps said, with a smirk.

The door to the bridge opened, and in walked Jess with Max in tow. "Holy cannoli!" Max exclaimed. "What a ship. She's a beauty! And she has cloaking ability!"

"But can you keep her running when in battle?" Eps asked.

"You bet your bottom dollar I can!"

"Good. Ship is on autopilot for Taurus-9. Let's go over our rescue plan."

\* \* \*

The crew assembled in the mess, waiting on Eps to start the briefing. "Crash, I assume you researched how we are going to get in, get Tamson, and get out, all in one piece, preferably undetected?" Eps wasn't above putting someone on the spot, especially if they already had an answer.

"Yes," Crash replied, a little nervousness in his voice. He didn't like the spotlight, but it was his sister, so he would have to man up and run the show.

"Well, please enlighten the rest of us."

"Okay, the prison sits on a plain, surrounded by kilometers of open barren country. Approach is virtually impossible."

"What about the cloaked shuttles?" Bear asked.

"We'd have to set them down somewhere and still penetrate the shields. The shields being used are old and were never upgraded. They cycle every so often because there is a hole in them. Actually, there are several holes. Each cycle, the holes move to a different spot."

"But the cycling is random, and the location of the holes are random," Bear pointed out.

"Ha," Crash said, with a big grin. "The manufacturer and the government want you to believe that. However, the truth is that the cycle time and location of the holes are actually based on a complex mathematical formula. Engineering couldn't get past the holes, so they introduced flux that made it appear random."

"And you know this how?" Max asked.

"As I said before, Tamson got a lot of sympathy from a wide array of fans. One of them is the guy who developed this shield. He gave me the formula and educated me on its use, with the caveat that it wasn't to be used except to rescue Tamson. Seems his kid was cured with a drug she came up with.

"In any event, I can use the formula with *Stingray*'s powerful computers to predict when and where the holes will form. From there, using the transporter, we beam a rescue team in, snatch Tamson, and beam out. Piece of cake."

"Rarely is a plan a 'piece of cake'," Eps retorted. "What happens if we miss the hole we beamed through?"

"I can tell where and when the next set of holes will be and guide you to them."

"Won't our COMM be blocked or picked up?" Bear asked.

"Nope. *Stingray*'s COMM can penetrate the shields. Frequencies we use won't be detected by the antiquated equipment in the prison," Crash responded.

"We still need a backup plan," Eps said.

"That's easy," Bear started. "If all else fails, *Stingray*'s cannon blasts the shields to crap, then takes out communications and weapons. Lock the transporter on y'all asses and beam you the hell out. And then we skedaddle!"

Everyone around the table chuckled. "Sounds like a fine plan," Eps said, dripping with sarcasm.

* * *

*Stingray* and her crew arrived in high orbit around Taurus-9. "We're cloaked, shields up 100%. Sensors show no other vessels in the area. Long range sensors are also clear, Captain," Jess reported. "I'm scanning the prison shielding and running the penetration program. It looks like there's a hole directly above the courtyard, three hundred meters up; another hole in the cafeteria?"

"A lot of times the hole will manifest itself as a buckling of the shield into a specific point," Crash answered. "We have to beam into one of these buckles in order to gain access."

"Once the shield cycles, won't we get zapped when the shield snaps back?" Bear asked.

"No," Max started to answer. "The shield does a reset, so in effect, the shield drops for just an instant, and new buckles and holes are calculated. Most of the holes are way too small for anything to get through, except maybe a low-level energy beam like the transporter. The trick is to beam through a hole into a buckle just a hair before the buckle collapses, leaving us there and intact."

"And beam out the same way?"

"Yes. But the good news is that there are also buckles with holes. That is the ideal scenario to look for. The success rate for that would be much higher!

"I've run some scenarios through the computer. Comparing that to the scans I've been taking, it looks like the formula is dead on."

"Crash, you said Tamson would be in the communal shower room shortly?" Eps asked.

"Yes," Crash answered. "Last time I visited her, I told her to find a way to linger there without supervision or prying eyes. She volunteered to do cleanup after their shower."

"Why did you pick that spot?"

"According to previous scenarios I ran, that area of the prison had the highest number of buckles with holes. And, when they appeared in this area, for some reason, they stayed the longest. Might be due to the high humidity, I don't know. Thirty minutes compared to five elsewhere. I even saw some buckles only stay around for a mere few seconds."

"Right then," Eps started. "Crash, you run the calcs from up here. Keep an eye out for visitors and make sure we don't get detected. Feed the coordinates to Jess down at the transporter console. Max, Bear, you're with me. Arm up and meet me at the transporter." Both Max and Bear nodded and headed down below.

"Captain, I really think I should go," Crash complained. "She won't know you."

Cutting him off, Eps responded, "This is your calculation. I need you here running it. Besides, she knows we're coming, right?" Crash nodded. "So, what could go wrong?" Eps smiled.

"She can be stubborn."

"So can I." Eps turned and headed below as well.

* * *

Epsilon, Max, and Bear were assembled on the transport platform. Jess, at the console, opened a channel to the bridge. "Smythe to Crash, we're all set."

"Roger that. Standby, sending coordinates to you now. It will materialize in an access shaft ten meters from the target. Doesn't look like Lady Luck is totally on our side. The shaft is horizontal, so the three of them will have to lay down, head-to-foot."

"Copy that. Sorry, guys. There's not enough room on the

platform to do that, so you are going to have to lie partially on top of each other."

"Oh, that is so gonna be awkward," Eps commented. The three of them laid down, staggering on top of each other.

"Too bad I don't have a vid recorder," Jess said, trying not to chuckle.

"Don't even go there, Smythe!" Eps scolded.

"Okay, Crash, ready," Jess said, ignoring Eps.

"Slaving transport to the program," Crash said. "Remember, keep your voices down and hold your position until I give the clear that the shields have reset. Okay, here we go, in three, two, one, energizing."

The three comrades left *Stingray* and materialized in the access shaft above and off to the side of the shower room. An awkward silence ensued; the only sounds heard were that of women showering only ten meters away. Max must have had that same thought as Eps felt something press into the back of his left thigh. *Wonderful.*

"Okay," Crash announced over the headset. "You are free to maneuver. Ten meters ahead there should be a service panel into the room."

"We're quite aware of where they are," Eps retorted, sarcastically. They inched forward, and Eps took the lead.

"Are there naked women showering right now?"

"Oh, yeah, baby. The likes of which…," Max replied, as his voice trailed off.

"Keep your collective eyes off my sister!" Crash yelled back.

As the three quietly approached the access panel, Eps could see three very attractive human females finishing up their shower, gabbing back and forth all the while. It wasn't hard to pick Tamson out. She was the only one whose hair looked like it was on fire. The picture Crash had didn't do her justice in the flesh. Eps couldn't wait to see her close-up.

Tamson was looking around, like she heard something, probably the buzz of the transport or maybe the shield cycling. She spotted Eps and instinctively covered up with her arms and was about to say something when Eps put a finger over his mouth and shook his head side-to-side. He pointed up, mouthing the word "Jimmy." She got it.

"Why are you covering yourself like that?" one of the women asked.

Snapping back to the present, Tamson replied, "Just got a chill all of a sudden." It was hard for her to drop her arms and fully expose her naked body to these strange men. As she did so, she turned and walked over to the rack, grabbed a towel, and wrapped herself up in it. Turning back to the other women she said, "Let's finish up so I can clean up. I'm beat."

"Here, I can help," the other woman said, still standing there naked.

"No, that's okay," Tamson said, grabbing towels and tossing it to the other two women. "You know how Matilda gets when you don't do things her way. In fact, she'll probably be here any minute screaming, 'You're still here and haven't even started cleaning yet?'."

"Yeah, you're right," she said, chuckling at Tamson's mockery. The two other women dried off and wrapped the towels around themselves as they exited the shower room.

"Captain, we have a problem," Eps heard Crash over his earpiece. "The hole just collapsed unexpectedly, standby."

Epsilon opened the access panel, dropped to the floor, and started walking toward Tamson. Max and Bear dropped out of the ceiling, taking up cover positions.

"Tamson, I presume? I'm Captain Epsilon, this is Max and Bear," Eps started quietly, motioning toward the other two while looking out through the door. "We're here on behalf of Crash to get you out."

"Up until you called him Crash, I thought you were some of the perverted guards," Tamson said.

Eps set the backpack he was carrying down and started pulling out clothes. "Here, Taz, lose the towel and put these on. Hurry, we don't have much time."

"INCOMING!" Max yelled. Laser bolts started flying into the room, both Max and Bear returned fire. Eps jumped on top of Taz, knocking her naked body to the ground just as she had started changing. Eps drew his pistol and returned fire as he had the best angle. He dropped two guards while the other two took cover. BOOM! Bear had thrown one of his "grenades" into the open doorway and, as promised, the opening was sealed shut. Laser shots could be heard outside.

"Don't worry," Bear, said. "They ain't coming through there."

"Sorry about that, Taz," Eps said, looking at her underneath him. He tried to cushion the force with one arm under her.

"My name is Tamson Alexandria Zubreé. You can call me Dr. Zubreé or Tamson! Now get off of me!" Taz shouted. Epsilon obliged. Damn, she was fine. China white skin over a toned and hard body, medium sized breasts with pink little nipples, shapely legs, blue eyes and fire red hair. "And stop staring at me!"

"Right, sorry," Eps said, chagrined as he got up and turned around.

"CAPTAIN!" Crash yelled in Epsilon's ear, causing him to wince a little.

"Crash, I need a way out, now! Where's the next hole?"

"Standby, we're getting another buckle—yes! With a hole in it. Looks like Lady Luck is definitely on our side. Fifteen meters behind where you beamed in, in the vertical shaft."

Turning back around, he found that she had pulled on the pants, shirt and boots that Eps brought in the backpack. "Right then, Taz it is. Let's go now!" Grabbing her arm, he steered her back to the access panel in the ceiling. "Max, you first." Eps made a step by putting his two hands together and interlocking his fingers. Max stepped into it and he hoisted him up and into the opening. "Taz, you're next." She followed Max's lead and was in through the opening, with Max grabbing her arms and helping her up and through. "Take her to the transport site," he told Max.

"Not leaving you, Captain."

"That's an order! Go! Bear, you're next."

"Negative, Captain. You're the senior officer, you go," Bear said, and hoisted Eps up and through the hole, catching him off guard. Just then the side of wall exploded, knocking Bear to the ground, sending debris into the room, and causing the crawl space to drop down a couple feet, almost sending Epsilon spilling back down into the room. Eps saw the guards coming through the opening and had an excellent bead on them. Without hesitation, he opened fire, dropping one guard after another. Silence followed.

"Come on Bear, give me your hand," Eps ordered, extending his arm down. A dazed Bear grabbed it and part jumping and part shear strength of Eps pulling, Bear came up and toppled on top of Eps in the damaged crawlspace, their faces mere inches from each other's. "This doesn't mean we are going to take long hot showers together, Bear!"

"You saved my life, Captain."

"Hrmph, we're not out of this yet. Get going." Bear got up and started crawling down the chase. Eps turned over in time to see two guards come in. Eps only had time to drop one guard as he started crawling forward. The other guard, firing wildly at Epsilon, charged in. One of the laser bolts connected with a strut holding the chase up. Consequently, the chase tipped more, and Eps slid down, which gave the guard an opportunity to grab Eps's ankle.

* * *

"Captain, the hole is disappearing, we have to go now!" Max yelled, as Bear arrived at the transport point, which was basically an outcropping in a vertical shaft with which the crawlspace intersected.

"Go now, all of you!" Eps yelled, as he kicked the gun out of the guard's other hand. Unfortunately, he didn't have a clear shot at him.

"We're not leaving you!" Bear yelled.

"Secure the package, that's an order!"

Hearing that over the COMM, Jess transported the three out of the access shaft. With a pop, the hole in the shield disappeared, leaving Epsilon behind.

The guard grabbed the catwalk with the other hand, trying to pull himself up. Eps let him get up just enough before kicking him hard in the face with his free boot. The guard let go and crumpled to the floor, blood oozing from his nose and mouth. He could hear more guards coming. Eps turned over and fast crawled to the extraction point. "Crash, at the extraction point, talk to me."

"Um," Crash started, "the hole dissipated. Calculating another hole near you, standby."

"I'm about to have company, hurry up!" Eps fired a couple shots at the remaining supports, bringing the catwalk down into a crumpled mess. "That should hold them off for a little bit," he mumbled to himself.

\* \* \*

"Crash! The captain's still down there! I need to know where another hole is going to materialize, and I need it NOW!" Jess yelled over the COMM at Crash.

"I'm working on it as fast as I can, Lieutenant! I'm also trying to jam outbound communication from the prison, but they're frequency hopping," Crash answered, stress very apparent in his voice.

"Target the COMSAT and destroy it. We're too far out for them to communicate with Command from the planet surface."

"Roger that," Crash said, relieved. He pulled up the targeting system, locked onto the communications satellite in orbit, and fired. A purple stream of light leapt out from *Stingray* and crashed into the satellite, obliterating it. "Satellite destroyed. I have Eps on the COMM, patching you in.

"Okay, Captain. Another hole should materialize shortly, about thirty meters up the shaft you are standing in front of."

\* \* \*

"Lovely," Eps quipped as he looked down the shaft. About

five meters down was a crisscross of red laser beams. Anyone falling into that would be instantly sliced and diced. Looking up, another set of a crisscross of lasers, about one hundred meters, Eps figured. He started climbing. About half-way up, he heard a blaster go off and felt the heat of the bolt fly by him, ending in a shower of sparks as it hit the laser beams above. "Oh, crap!"

"Eps, what's your status?" Jess asked Eps over the COMM.

"I have company!" Eps answered as he returned fire, hitting the guard in the shoulder, causing him to lose his balance and fall right into the laser bed. There wasn't much of him left as he passed through it. Eps continued his climb up. As he reached the next platform, he had to expose a little more of himself and this time the laser bolt connected along his left side. "AHHHHH, I'm hit!"

\* \* \*

"Eps!" Jess yelled over the COMM. She was greeted with silence.

"Send me back! I'll get him!" Bear yelled, jumping up on the platform.

"No, get off. You're too heavy. The hole is materializing in the middle of the shaft. Max, take the console. Crash give me coordinates on the top part of the hole. I'm going to get a running jump as I beam over so I can hit the platform Eps is on. I'll grab Eps, jump back, and beam us out at the bottom of the hole. Bear, give me your gun." Bear complied. Jess had her gun in one hand and Bear's in the other, both pointed down.

"Lieutenant, the timing has to be perfect. Otherwise you are both dead!" Crash said, emphatically.

"Well, then, I guess you and Max better get it perfect. Okay, I'm ready, say the word." Jess positioned herself off the platform, in a runner's start stance.

"Ready, set, GO!" Crash screamed.

\* \* \*

Epsilon was lying on the platform, out of the line of fire. He could hear guards trying to climb up the shaft, just huffing and puffing. He was really glad the tradition of eating donuts was passed down from one generation of guards to another. This was one of the vices Earth passed on to the rest of the universe.

He was momentarily drawn away from the pain in his side, not sure if what he was seeing was real or a hallucination. But all of a sudden, a strikingly beautiful woman, who looked remarkably like Jessie Smythe, materialized out of thin air, a gun in each hand, shooting wildly down below. He heard screams as several guards fell through the bed of lasers, meeting their instant demise.

"'Bout time you showed up," was all that Eps could muster before he passed out.

"Stay with me, Reggie!" Jess said, holstering her weapon and grabbing his collar. "Crash, Max, you ready?"

"Transporter ready," Max replied.

"I have you locked, go, Crash said.

"Here we come!" Jess yelled. She grabbed Eps with her free hand and with all her might, she dragged and pushed him over the edge of the platform and into the hole. As they descended, she fired wildly with Bear's gun in her free hand.

* * *

The two re-materialized on *Stingray* and fell uncontrollably into a heap just off the platform. Bear and Taz ran over immediately to him. "Get him to sickbay!" Taz ordered. "You do have a sickbay, right?"

"Yes, we do," Bear replied, picking up Epsilon. "Follow me!" He headed out the door and down the corridor to sickbay, gingerly plopping him down on a table. Taz and Jess were right behind, followed by Max.

While Taz quickly familiarized herself with the layout of the instruments, Jess hit the COMM on the wall. "Smythe to Crash, get us out of here and put us someplace safe."

"Aye, Lieutenant," came Crash's response. "Is he alive?"

"Barely," she replied, and killed the COMM.

Taz quickly cut Eps's shirt off. A long, black, charred streak enveloped his entire left side. She cut his pants off. The charring went from just below his left hip up to his left armpit. "Damn," was all she said, and then looked up at the monitor. "His vitals are critical but WOW, they're surprisingly stable." She grabbed a portable scanner and laser scalpel and started scanning and removing tissue. "What the...?" her voice trailed off.

Realizing that Taz would soon figure out what was happening, Jess barked out, "OKAY, everyone out. Give the doc room to work. That's an order!" Jess physically ushered everyone out. She hit a button near the door and secured it. Jess briskly walked over to Taz, who was standing there dumbfounded.

"Five percent of the charring has already healed," Taz started, with an incredulous look on her face. "His internal organs are regenerating themselves repairing the damage. That's—"

Jess grabbed Taz and forcibly shoved her into the wall. "You're a smart woman, doctor. You are going to figure out what is happening if you haven't already. You probably have but don't want to believe it because the medical community says it's impossible. Nevertheless, here we are, and it is happening in front of your eyes.

"Epsilon has gone to great lengths to keep this a secret. Only two people in the entire universe know it. You are now number three and you will take it to your grave. There will be no discussing it at conferences; there will be no papers written on it; you will not breathe a word of it to anyone, not even to your brother. If you do, I will personally kill you, do you understand?" Taz nodded. She was good at reading people and knew Jess was more than capable of making good on her promise. She also knew that Jess was tightly wound right now. "Excellent."

"I really wish women would stop fighting over me," Eps croaked out. "It really is disconcerting."

Jess was at his bedside before he finished, putting her hand on top of his. "How are you feeling?"

"Like I got run over by a Pungdon Bull."

"Lieutenant, the Captain needs his rest," Taz said forcibly, as she regained her composure and opened the door to sickbay. "You need to leave."

"Jess," Eps started, weakly, "execute program zeta326 in the NAV system."

"Aye, Captain." Jess gave Eps's hand a squeeze before letting go and walked out of sickbay. A few moments later, Eps could feel *Stingray* change course.

Taz walked over to Eps. They stared at each other for a long moment. "Thanks, doc," Eps finally said.

"It was all you. I didn't really do anything," Taz replied, indignantly. She didn't like being bested by someone else, especially a non-medical somebody.

"Yes, you did. If nothing else, you cared. That means more to a patient than anything else."

Taz looked away, tears welling up in her eyes. She knew he was spot on. "You cared too—enough to—sort of—risk your life to rescue me. Thank you."

"Well, I couldn't let an injustice go unpunished, now could I?" Eps said, smiling. Taz cracked a little bit of a smile. "I can die, you know, just not very easily. I came very close one time; and it hurt like a some-bitch; something I'm not too keen on doing again."

Taz couldn't help but to chuckle. "Your secret is safe with me, Captain. I promise. Though I AM intrigued and can't promise that I won't keep investigating the...," Taz was searching for the perfect words. "Precipitating factors of your—um—medical anomaly."

"Well, that's good enough for me. Thanks."

She nodded. "Get some rest. Doctor's orders." She looked around sickbay.

"That's your office over there," Eps motioned to the door on a side wall. "Your private quarters are through the far door in the office."

"Got it, thanks." She dimmed the lights and headed into her office. *Oh, how I've missed having my OWN office. And more importantly, my own PRIVATE quarters!*

## CHAPTER FIVE

Max and Bear were sitting around the table in the mess, eating and drinking when Crash walked in, relief showing on his face.

"So, is your sister currently seeing anyone?" Max asked, with a huge grin on his face.

"Hey, my sister's off limits!" Crash exclaimed, with a dead serious look. He walked over to the food replicator, punched some buttons, and out came two dishes and drinks.

"Where IS the little lady?" Max asked, eying the two plates of food Crash had.

"She's checking on Eps," he growled, as Taz walked in and sat down next to her brother.

"Where's Jess?" Taz asked.

"She's on the bridge," Crash replied.

"Listen," Taz started, "I want to thank you all for risking your lives to rescue me."

"Oh, think nothing of it," Max said, with a grin. "Besides, your big brother here was driving us nuts. Kept pulling out that picture of you and pining about his duty to get you out of that mess. Blah, blah, blah. Me? I was just curious to see if you looked like your picture in person."

"Oh, really?" Taz asked. "And the verdict?"

Max rested his elbow on the table and his chin on his hand and looked longingly at Taz. "Oh—yeah—baby!"

Taz smiled, looked down and blushed a little.

"Enough!" Crashed yelled. He was clearly distressed at the prospect of his baby sister getting involved with any man, let alone one of these guys.

"So, Jimmy, you served with Epsilon and Jess. What's their story?" Taz asked, purposefully changing the subject.

"Yeah, what's their deal?" Bear chimed in.

Crash welcomed the subject change away from his sister. "Well, it all started during the Mech War. Eps was captain of the AWS *Freedom* and I was her chief helmsman. We had intel on the location of the Mech's Central Command. As you remember, all the Mechs were connected by some sub-space COMM that we could never hack into. All their attacks were coordinated, and that was why they were so effective. We found out by accident that EMP would disrupt their COMM for a short time."

"What's EMP?" Taz asked.

"EMP stands for Electro Magnetic Pulse. It's a by-product of a nuclear explosion," Max chimed in, smiling at Taz.

"Right—" Crash continued, giving Max a wry look. "So, while their COMM was disrupted, they were disconnected, were lost and would just shut down. In that state, we could pick them off easily. But generating an EMP strong enough required, as Max said, detonating a nuclear explosion. It was going to cause as much damage as the damned Mechs did. So, we figured if we could take out their central command, all the Mechs would be disconnected. We'd mop 'em up and end the war."

"Yeah, that's history. We heard their central command was destroyed, but it was oddly swept under the rug," Bear said.

"I know. That was us. Well, really, it was Eps and Jess. Then there was the cover up." Both Max and Bear's eyes got big.

"Let me set the stage for you. The Mech's Central Command was not located on their home world. It was actually on a deserted planet. There were no orbital defenses and no troops on the ground, just a minimal security force. Central Command was protected by a single bunker and a ridge. Brilliant, actually; I guess they figured we weren't smart enough to look for them there and if we did stumble upon them, they could cut us down. From the bunker, they could take out any approach by land or air. We got the *Freedom* close to this planet, staying behind one of the moons so we wouldn't be detected. Since an orbital detector would have given them away, they could only detect us from the ground. We figured a small shuttle inbound on the far side of the planet would go undetected. We had two marine fire teams onboard. We planned to put one of the teams on the ground, and they would take out the bunker. The key was to get to them before they raised their shields. Otherwise, we would be totally screwed."

"They kept their shields down?" Bear asked.

"Yep. If they kept them raised, sensors from passing ships would detect them. Anyway, Eps knew that it was a bad plan, but it was the only plan the Alliance had. The first shuttle went in undetected. We detected heavy fire, but they never raised their shields. We figured they got close but failed. The Mechs followed a very logical thought process. You could stand right in front of them all day long and if you were not a threat, they would ignore you. To them, acting on a non-threat was a waste of resource. But mind you, the nanosecond they deemed you a threat, they'd cut you down without any emotion.

"Anyway, once the first team missed their second call-in, we knew they were all dead. Alliance Command ordered Eps to send in the second team, over his protests."

"They should have just sent all our cruisers to the planet and obliterated it," Max said.

"Well, that was a thought. But AOA strategists realized that was too easy. Our cruisers would be detected long before they arrived, prompting the Mechs to raise their shields. Our strategists also feared that there were many more defensive weapons hidden deep underground and would be undetectable to us from a distance. It would be the perfect scenario for the Mechs. Stupid humans would send everything we had to the planet, only to be totally wiped out as we arrived in orbit.

"Anyway, I was the pilot of the second shuttle. We decided to do a HALO drop right on top of the bunker."

"HALO?" Taz asked.

"High Altitude, Low Opening parachute drop. Eps figured that single, small objects falling would be construed as a non-threat. The planet was regularly bombarded by small asteroids, so the Mechs were hopefully numb to it.

"Unfortunately, they detected the shuttle. Guess they were expecting another attack. Maybe we didn't wait long enough. I don't know. Our port engine and stabilizer were hit. I was able to hold the shuttle together long enough for the fire team to jump, but they landed too far from the target. By the time I jumped, I ended up landing smack dab in the middle, right between the far ridge and the bunker. I broke my leg on landing. I guess, fortunately for me, they deemed me a non-threat because I was wounded. I don't know how long I was lying there, blacking out from the pain, but I saw movement out of the corner of my eye in the break in the ridge. It was Epsilon. He motioned for me to stay put; like I was going anywhere...."

* * *

Onboard the *Freedom*, everyone on the bridge gasped when they detected the shuttle being hit. Silence and gloom came over all of them when it crashed and exploded a few moments later. "Jacobs, you have the CONN," Eps said, breaking the silence.

"Aye sir," Jacobs replied, taking the command chair as Eps headed for the turbo lift. "What's the plan, Captain?"

"I'm going after them. If you don't hear from me in twelve hours, execute a retreat behind the moon and report back to Alliance Command," Eps answered his XO.

"But Captain, there are no shuttles left."

"I don't need one. I'm going down in a XR-30 Combat Suit."

"It's a prototype. It hasn't been fully tested yet."

"Can't think of a better test scenario. Can you?"

"Captain, even if you make it to the planet surface, all your fuel and power will have been depleted," started Harkins, the chief engineer of the *Freedom*. "How will you get back?"

"Well, if I destroy the bunker, you can come and get me. Otherwise, the first shuttle is still intact. Jacobs, have the Master-At-Arms meet me in the hanger with two Mark-5 plasma bunker busters."

"Aye, Captain," Jacobs responded with raised eyebrows as Eps disappeared in the turbo lift. The Mark-5 was a newly developed weapon, its design was based on very old-school tactics of being propelled by a rocket. Since it was considered a payload, it could be deployed in a multitude of ways, including equipping it with a hardened cone to penetrate unshielded fortifications.

* * *

Eps was greeted in the hangar by Maxwell, the Master-At-Arms of the ship. Word spread quickly of the captain's rescue plan and a half dozen or so crew members were in the hanger eager to lend a hand. More were hovering in the corridor. They knew that if it were one of them down there, the Old Man would be doing the same thing for them. Besides, anyone who was ever under Eps's command fully respected him. He earned it immediately, not only with "stunts" (as the brass would call it) like this, but he treated each crew member with respect. He firmly believed to command one's respect you first had to give it.

"Captain," Maxwell saluted, as Eps walked in and saluted back. "Two Mark-5's as requested. Also took the liberty of securing a backpack, rations, water and a med kit."

"Chief, no one can deny that you are thorough! Thank you," Eps said, walking over to the locker that contained the XR-30 suit.

"I'll get that for you Captain," Harkins said, grabbing the handle. Eps was always amazed how he could leave before him, but Harkins was always there waiting. "Can't have you burn up during entry on my watch, sir."

"Much obliged, as I'd prefer not to burn up either."

Harkins and two other mates helped Eps into the suit while Harkins gave him the "Combat Suit and Mark-5 for Dummies" quickie refresher. Once in, the helmet was twisted on and he was guided over to the airlock, ready for his extravehicular activity (EVA). One of the mates grabbed the portable life support pack that was attached to the suit through an umbilical cord and carried it for his captain.

"Eps to Jacobs," Eps announced, over the COMM in the headset.

"Jacobs here, sir. Read you 5-by-5."

"Roger that. Same here." Eps was standing at the inside airlock hatch. Harkins hit the open button, and the door slid open. He detached the umbilical and held it up for Eps to see. Eps gave him the thumbs-up and stepped in.

"I'm reading an open inside hatch, airlock one," Jacobs said.

"Affirmative," Eps responded as he pressed the close button. "Ready for EVA." He pressed the depressurize button and even through the suit, Eps could hear the hiss of the air escaping the chamber.

"Airlock depressurized. You are a go for EVA."

Eps pressed the open button for the outer door and it slid open.

"I'm reading open exterior hatch, airlock one."

"Affirmative." The airlock was located at the rear of the ship. Eps stepped out, still holding the assist rail.

"Is there a problem, Captain?" Harkins asked. He hoped Eps was getting cold feet. This was a suicide mission.

"Negative," Eps responded. "Jacobs, give me an opening in the shields around me. I want you to sharply swing the ass-end of the ship toward the planet to give me a launch-off. You might get detected, so afterward tuck yourself into a crevice and go dark for a little bit."

"Aye, Captain. Godspeed and see you on the return," Jacobs said, with as much sincerity as he could muster. Jacobs secretly hoped Epsilon would be killed in this mission, so he would assume command of the *Freedom*. He firmly believed that he was better than Eps. In fact, he believed himself to be better than anybody else on this ship, and that he should be Captain and not some lowly Lt. Commander. He offered just enough rebuke to show concern and then was more than happy to support Epsilon in his death mission. On the flip side, he knew that the crew would only accept him as their commander if Epsilon were dead.

"Roger that," Eps responded.

"Okay, here we go. Kick off on my mark. Three, two, one, MARK!" The *Freedom* swung hard around and Eps jumped, propelling him toward the planet. Timing was perfect as Eps only had to minimally use the suit's thrusters to execute minor course corrections. He spotted a small drone (too small to have been picked up on sensors) meandering ahead and slightly to the right of him. It abruptly changed course and headed toward where he came from. To the drone, he just looked like another piece of space debris floating about. Switching to his rear sensor, he could see no sign of *Freedom*. Jacobs was a capable officer—capable of saving his own ass, that is—so he had no doubt he followed his orders to the tee and *Freedom* was sitting dark in some crevice of the moon.

The point Eps would be most exposed was during entry. Even though he offered a small profile, he still would flame when he entered the atmosphere. The suit would absorb ninety-nine percent of the heat, but from the ground, he would look like a small meteorite entering the atmosphere. Since this planet is bombarded daily, he was counting on the Mechs to be a little complacent in that area. Besides, how much of a threat is one human in a space suit, anyway? He was counting on that "logic" to help him out.

* * *

Breaking through the upper atmosphere was uneventful. The suit performed flawlessly. As he descended, he locked onto the first shuttle. It had landed without a scratch, so that's where he decided to head. Just then, a beep lit up the screen. He located Crash. He was alive, but injured, and smack dab in the middle of Mech Central Command. *Great!* Now the tricky part: he'd have to pull some massive G's by slowing down at the last minute. If he started slowing now, the Mechs would become suspicious. Meteorites typically hit the ground full bore. That is what he was going to do, at least until he was over the ridge line hiding the shuttle.

As he approached the ridge, he toggled open the cap that was covering the emergency jettison button. Clearing the ridge, with only six hundred meters until impact, he hit the red button. Downward thrusters ignited with full force, making it seem like he ran into a brick wall, but he was still descending at a maddening speed. At three hundred meters, the explosive bolts blew, and the suit came apart into several pieces, going in all different directions lightening the load; only the jet pack remained. At two hundred meters, a parachute deployed. Using compressed gas to rapidly place the chute into optimal braking position, the thrusters went silent and ran out of fuel.

The landing was rough. How could it not be? But he knew how to land in rough conditions and while not breaking any bones, all of his innards were violently jarred around. However, he was spot on, one hundred meters from the shuttle. Eps removed the chute pack, gathered it up into a bundle and stowed it in the back of the shuttle. He then hoisted his pack onto his back, grabbed a laser rifle from the weapons locker on the shuttle, and headed off toward Mech Central Command.

* * *

Epsilon arrived at the ridge protecting the bunker and stopped at the small break in it. Poking his head around edge, he could see a man lying on the ground, his left leg bent at a hideous angle. "Psssst," Eps uttered. Slowly, Jimmy "Crash"

Zubreé turned his head toward the sound. Even from this distance, Eps could see his face light up. "Shh," Eps mouthed, putting his index finger over his lips. Crash gave the slightest nod and turned his head back to its original position. Eps thought he detected voices and/or movement. Scrambling forward five hundred meters, he took up a position on the forward edge of the ridge where he found another break. Peering in, he could see that the bunker had large laser cannons recessed inside it. He could also see the members of the first fire team. Their bodies were nothing more than a gory, twisted mess. They didn't see the emplacement, dug into the top of the ridge. From that vantage point, the Mechs could cut down anyone and anything coming through or over the ridge. It was an unbelievably strategic spot.

Hearing footsteps again, Eps turned to see the second fire team coming around the ridge. "Glad to see you made it, Lieutenant," Eps whispered.

"Captain, what are doing on the ground?" Lt. JG McCully asked.

"Came down here to save your sorry behinds. Zubreé is in the middle of that," Eps said, nodding towards the other side of the ridge. "He's alive but injured."

"Well, sir, we'll take out that bunker and then we can secure him back to the *Freedom*."

"Negative," Eps ordered. "Up along that ridge is a gun emplacement, recessed into the rock wall. From that vantage point they will have you targeted before you can spot it. I have a better way, around the other side of the ridge."

"Sorry, sir, but I have my orders to take that bunker."

"Understood, but I outrank you and am giving you new orders," Eps said, with as much sarcasm as possible. He met McCully a couple times. He fingered him as a pompous ass and certainly not a team player. He was all about the glory.

"I beg to differ, sir. My orders came direct from the Admiralty. Therefore, unless you intend to shoot me, we are moving out."

"Shooting you would only give away our position. Suit yourself." Eps stepped back and sat down, with his back to the ridge. He watched as the team moved forward to his left into the break. Nothing happened. As the last person in the column passed by him, he noticed she was lagging a few feet behind the man in front of her. On impulse, he grabbed her rucksack from behind, pulled her back and slammed her down into the dirt on his right side, just as the last man disappeared around the break. Eps grabbed the female soldier again, threw her face down in the dirt and rolled on top of her, just as the big laser cannons opened up. Even though the ridge was six hundred meters tall, pieces of earth and body parts flew over the ridge and on top of them. The ground shook so violently that Eps was bounced off of the soldier. It was over just as quickly as it started; those massive weapons just chewed the marines to bits.

Straightening up, Epsilon asked, "What is your name, soldier?"

"Smythe, Jessie, Corporal, sir," the female soldier responded, shakily. "Thank you, sir, for saving my life."

"It ain't saved yet, Smythe," Eps chuckled. "We still have a mission to finish if you want to get out of here alive."

"But they cut them down just like you said."

"Oh, we're not going in the front door. We're going in the back door. It's only guarded by two Mechs. Saw it from the air. Let's go," he said, as he stood up. He headed back around the ridge where he came from. Smythe dutifully followed. She may have been green, but she was a quick learner and what she just learned was that the safest spot in a fight was right behind this guy.

As they approached the ridge, Eps could see Jimmy still laying there. They caught each other's eye and Eps gave a reassuring smile and thumbs-up gesture. Then he headed around and up the ridge, with Jessie in tow.

\* \* \*

Epsilon and Smythe summitted the ridge about five hundred meters from the bunker. Not a single Mech in sight. Their "logic" dictated that no one would (or could) be there without being spotted. Therefore, their logic also dictated that there was no need to expend resources guarding it. About thirty meters from the top edge of the bunker, Eps motioned to drop packs. He removed the two Mark-5's and Jessie's eyes lit up. "You know what these are?" he whispered.

"Yes sir," she whispered back.

"You know how to use 'em?"

"Yes sir. I just completed advanced munitions training and the Mark-5 was covered extensively."

"Good, because I didn't pay a damned bit of attention to what Harkins was saying," he paused. "You repeat that to him, and I'll kill you!"

"NO, SIR!" Jessie said, eyes wide.

"Joking, Smythe. Anyway, I am going to distract the two guards at the door. You set a twenty-second fuse on those things and toss them in the door."

"Yes sir," she said, fumbling with rocker switches on the bombs, setting the fuse.

"Can you do that?"

Jessie looked at the hatches and then looked at Eps. "Hopefully, they're not locked."

"That's the spirit," he slapped her on her back. "If it is locked, blast the upper right corner of it. That's where they 'hid' the locking mechanism. I want you to arm, open, and toss one to the left and the other down the shaft to the right. Close the door, latch it, and blast the lower and upper middle sections of the door. You have to complete it in less than fifteen seconds or we're dead. Understand?"

She nodded. "Why blast the upper and lower middle of the lid? How do you know all these details about Mech Central Command?"

"There's a metal retaining lip in those places. The heat will fuse them, trapping the Mechs inside long enough for the Mark-5's to detonate." He ignored her last question.

Jessie nodded. Eps got into position, spying the two guards. He looked back at Jess and circled his finger in the air. She nodded and took up a position right behind him.

Eps turned back and jumped, grabbing both guards with outstretched arms. All three went down in a heap of grinding metal on metal and rock.

Jess jumped right behind him, hitting the arming buttons while still in mid-air.

Wasting no time, he put his left foot on one side of the closest Mech's head and kicked with all might. His right foot came down square in the middle of its neck, severing it cleanly off and shutting it down.

Jess had the door open in no time flat; it wasn't locked.

The other Mech started crawling toward Eps. He jumped on top of it and using his bare hands, twisted its head three hundred sixty degrees around, snapping its neck and rendering it useless.

Jess heard the resonance of metal grinding on metal and rock, just as she finished dropping the second Mark-5. She was closing the door as Eps dragged both lifeless bodies and piled them up against it. "That should hold 'em for a little bit," he said, as they both blasted the door.

"What now?" she yelled.

"RUN!" Eps ordered, as he scrambled back up to the top of the ridge. They both grabbed their packs and were sprinting down the far side of the ridge as the bunker erupted in a spectacular blue, orange, and yellow fireball. They felt the heat before the shock wave hit them, propelling them down the side of the ridge head over heels. Fortunately, they were below the explosion, so they escaped without being vaporized.

* * *

"So," Crash continued, "Eps and Jess destroyed Mech Central Command. Each and every Mech and Mech ship came to a screeching halt. They were just sitting there, dumbfounded, not knowing what to do. Our Marines had a field day. Shooting one, blowing another one up. Since the Mech ships had no helm direction, they just drifted. Some ran into each other, erupting into breathtaking fireballs. We quickly figured out that even though we couldn't penetrate their shields, we could use our tractor beams in reverse and push them into each other or into the planet's atmosphere. Either way, that day, every single Mech was destroyed."

"Eventually, Eps and Jess retrieved the shuttle, picked me up, and rendezvoused with *Freedom*. Doc fixed my leg up. There was a lot of rejoicing on the ship, except, as I now recall, the XO didn't seem too happy to see his Captain. We returned to port for some much-needed R&R. Unfortunately, I got summoned to appear as a witness in a court martial of Corporal Smythe. She was being charged with dereliction of duties. Specifically, for not following the orders of her commanding officer. Personally, I think Jacobs had something to do with it. Admiral Roth was hell bent on pinning those deaths on her since Eps was a hero and he was untouchable at the time. He received the medal of honor, as did Jess, but with a lot less fanfare. After all, he was a captain and she a lowly female corporal…."

* * *

"These proceedings shall come to order, the honorable Admiral John T. Carlisle presiding. All may be seated," the bailiff said. "Your honor, this is the case in the matter of Alliance Command vs. Corporal Jessie Smythe. The accused is being charged with dereliction of duties for not obeying orders."

"Your honor," the prosecutor started, "we intend to show—"

"Stow it, Lieutenant," Carlisle ordered. "Let me get this straight. You are charging this soldier with disobeying an order, the same order that led to two fire teams being cut down?"

"Yes sir," he said, tentatively.

"Corporal, according to your response, your team was ordered by Captain Reginald Epsilon, command AWS *Freedom,* to not take the bunker from the front, but to follow his plan to take it from the rear. Is that correct?"

"Yes, sir," Corporal Smythe said, as she stood.

"Objection, your honor," the prosecutor said. "That's hearsay. Captain Epsilon is not here."

"Defense, why is the captain not on the witness list?" Carlisle asked, quite irritated.

"Your honor," the defense attorney said, as he stood. "We attempted to subpoena Captain Epsilon but were told he was unavailable and could not be reached."

"And who told you this?"

"Admiral Roth, sir."

Carlisle wrinkled his nose and turned a slight shade of magenta at the mention of Roth's name and his meddling in his court's affairs. "Hmm," was all he said.

Just then, the doors burst open and in walked Captain Epsilon, in full military uniform, sporting the Medal of Honor. "Pardon the interruption, Admiral. The *Freedom* has been ordered to sail immediately for the Nubia system; pirates are attacking supply ships as well as some targets on the planet surface."

"And how, Captain, does that involve these proceedings?" Carlisle asked.

"You have my pilot, Ensign Jimmy Zubreé as a witness, sir. I can't leave without him. If it will please the court, I would like to offer testimony that I think will clear up this whole matter."

"Objection, your honor," the prosecutor started. "Captain Epsilon is not on the witness list."

"Overruled, counselor. It's obvious to me that the good captain here is not on some supersecret mission, that he couldn't spare the time to testify in MY court! Please enlighten us Captain and be quick about it."

"Yes sir. I don't wish to speak ill of the dead, sir, but I ordered the lieutenant to stand down, and that I had another plan. He disregarded my order and led his team straight into a known ambush. Corporal Smythe was the last one in the column. I grabbed her and told her she was with me as I could use a second body to increase the odds of a successful outcome. She followed my command and, well, sir, the rest is history, as they say.

"Furthermore, sir, as I stated in my report, Corporal Smythe performed above and beyond all expectations. She should be promoted, not this," Eps spread out his arms, taking in the entire courtroom.

"REPORT?" bellowed the admiral. "Why isn't that report included in the court documents?"

"Your honor," the defense attorney said. "Once again, my subpoena for said report was denied."

"Hrmph!"

* * *

"The admiral agreed," Crash continued, "and dismissed all charges against Jessie. She was promoted to Lieutenant Junior Grade (though I heard Roth had something to do with keeping her from getting full Lieutenant). Roth had her assigned as XO to Supply Outpost 259, literally in the middle of nowhere. The final piece to the story happened about six months later when we rendezvoused with an unmarked shuttle and took her into our bay. Her occupants were sequestered under Marine guard. Lt. Jacobs didn't even know what was up, which irritated him to no end. I was on duty when Eps came on the bridge...."

* * *

"Captain on the deck," Jacobs bellowed, as he vacated the command chair. He liked announcing the captain, particularly since Epsilon hated it. Jacobs decided that he would require it from his own deck crew once he had his own command.

"Helm, lay in a course for Supply Outpost 259, full speed," Eps barked, as he sat down in the command chair.

"Supply Outpost 259, aye sir," Crash responded. "Full speed ahead."

"Sir," Jacobs started, "what's going on? Who came aboard?"

Ignoring the question, Eps turned to the communications officer. "Lieutenant institute a complete COMM blackout effective immediately. No outbound communication without my explicit order."

"Aye, sir," the communications officer said, as she pushed a sequence of buttons, securing all outbound communications.

"We've been ordered," Eps started, as he turned back to Jacobs, "to take into custody Lt. Bristol, commanding officer of Supply Outpost 259. He is being charged with theft and sale of Alliance supplies, bullying junior officers, and a plethora of other charges that I really don't care about."

"Sir, we don't have the authority to arrest anyone."

"That is correct. However, I have been given a general order by Alliance Command to detain the Lt. and turn him over to the Alliance Marshals, who just happen to have come aboard recently."

"Oh. Very well, sir, I'll assemble a security detail."

"No need, Colonel Franks has a detail of

Marines to handle this."

"Marines? Expecting trouble?"

"Yes. Appears Bristol is not alone. I've been told he has loyal followers in the outpost's security force, and we may face some resistance."

\* \* \*

"We're being hailed, Captain," Jacobs reported as *Freedom* approached Outpost 259.

"On screen," Eps ordered.

An image of Lt. Bristol appeared. "Capt. Epsilon, while it is an honor to have you and the *Freedom* here, I don't have your arrival orders."

"We're ferrying additional parts for the AWS *Manoa* which is due in three days. It was a last-minute request by Command as we were the closest vessel to lend a hand. I'm sending two shuttles over. Some of my officers have never been on an outpost and requested the opportunity. Now they can say they were." Eps shrugged while chuckling.

"This is highly irregular, but very well. Use bay three."

"Bay three, thank you." Eps killed the connection.

Col. Franks emerged from the shadows, slightly startling Jacobs. "Captain, I have two teams of Marines in shuttles ready to go. I'll be in shuttle two and you in shuttle one. I'll deploy hard after you exit with Sgt. Krell's team."

"With all due respect, Captain," Jacobs started. "You should not be going on this mission. The XO of the ship should stand in, especially since it is a combat situation, sir." Jacobs wasn't going to miss an opportunity to shine and Eps knew it.

"You want to go?" Eps asked, after a pause. "Very well, you can come along too. Maybe you'll learn something for when you get your own command, Jacobs." That just fueled Jacobs's ego, and it showed by the huge smirk on his face.

* * *

The two shuttles settled into Outpost 259's bay three. Shuttle one lowered her ramp and Epsilon, Jacobs and a half dozen marines emerged. They were greeted by Lt. Bristol, his XO Lt. Smythe, and a half dozen security personnel, laser rifles aimed at them.

"Bristol!" Eps exclaimed. "What the hell is this?"

Quietly, Col. Franks and eight of his marines exited shuttle two from a hatch on the opposite side of the craft. They, along with the six marines behind Epsilon, quickly surrounded the security guards, who looked nervous and confused. Bristol and Smythe were the only ones who didn't draw on the landing party.

"What the—" It was now Bristol's turn to question the events at hand.

Epsilon brought up the tablet he was holding and tapped it. "General Order number 956-344, Lt. Bristol, you are hereby relieved of command of Supply Outpost 259, effective immediately. Furthermore, you are to surrender to command, AWS *Freedom*, where you will be turned over to Alliance Marshals and returned to Command, pending further investigation."

"Investigation? For what?" Bristol asked.

"I wasn't told. These are my orders. Chief of Security, you and your men have a choice to make.

Stand down or go down."

The security chief hesitantly looked at Bristol, then at the marines, then back to Eps. "Captain, the Lieutenant ordered us to defend the outpost from hostile forces. You don't look like hostile forces, sir." Lowering his rifle, he turned to his men and uttered, "Stand down." The half-dozen men lowered their weapons. The Marines didn't.

"Excellent choice, gentlemen," Eps said. Jacobs motioned to one of the Marines and the two of them took Bristol into custody and headed back into the shuttle. "Not so fast, Jacobs; I'm not finished." Jacobs came back out. Eps tapped the tablet again. "General Order number 956-345, Lt. Jacobs, you are hereby relieved as Executive Officer, AWS *Freedom* and will assume command of Supply Outpost 259, effective immediately. Congratulations, Lieutenant, you now have a command of your own, just what you wanted!"

"Captain!" Jacobs exclaimed. The faintest of snickers passed over the faces of the Marines, but one would have had to look really hard to see it. Everyone on *Freedom* knew Jacobs was gunning for the Old Man's job. Only Jacobs didn't know that everyone else knew, and now the table was turned.

Eps turned to the outpost XO. "Hello Jessie, good to see you. How have you been?"

"Hanging in there, sir," Jess answered. "It's good seeing you too." Eps could sense she was down about being passed over for the command slot and from the sounds of it, not too keen on getting a new boss.

Eps tapped the tablet again. "General Order number 956-346, Lt. JG, Smythe, you are hereby promoted to the rank of full lieutenant. Step forward." As she did, Eps tucked the tablet under

his arm and dug out two sets of double silver bars
from his pocket. He removed the single set of bars
from Jessie's uniform and pinned the new insignias
to her collar. He stepped back and saluted. Lt. Jessie
Smythe returned the salute. Stepping forward again,
he shook her hand and said, "Congratulations,
Lieutenant. You deserve it." Everyone except
Bristol and Jacobs started clapping. The Marines
finally stood down but kept a wary eye on the
security team and Jacobs.

"Thank you, sir," she replied.

Looking back at the tablet, Eps continued,
"Furthermore, you are hereby relieved as Executive
Officer, Supply Outpost 259 effective
immediately." Bewilderment replaced the surprised
expression on her face. "You are to report forthwith
to command, AWS *Freedom,* and assume the post
of her Executive Officer. Your commission starts
now, Smythe. Go pack your shit! Shuttle leaves in
ten."

"YES SIR!" Jess exclaimed, the biggest grin
on her face. She saluted and ran off to her quarters
to pack. She was stoked to be serving under Epsilon
and wasn't going to miss the shuttle off of this tin
can. And promoted to Lieutenant and XO to boot!

Turning back to Jacobs, Epsilon's demeanor
turned stone cold. "Don't think for a minute I didn't
know what you were up to. You want a command?
Now you have a command of your own. I'm sure
the chief of security here will be a fine asset and
happy to show you around your new home. Alliance
Command will expect recommendations for an XO
replacement. Don't get caught up like Bristol did
and you may just make it through this. Now—GET
THE HELL OFF OF MY SHUTTLE!"

Jacobs meekly walked off the shuttle onto

the outpost hangar deck. "What about my personal effects, SIR?"

"Colonel!" Eps answered.

"With pleasure, Captain," Franks replied, as he emerged from the other shuttle's rear door with two duffel bags. Another Marine was behind him carrying a box. They tossed them all on the deck.

* * *

"And that, my friends," Crash concluded, "is the story of how Eps and Jess came to be. She was his XO right up until the Alliance fell. It had to be one of the hardest moves for Eps to walk away from us without a word, but it should have been the safest move for everyone involved."

"Except look how it turned out for the lieutenant's family," Bear said.

Suddenly, *Stingray* dropped out of wave drive and shuddered. The lights throughout the entire ship went out amid the sounds of explosions from the engine room and the bridge. Alarms could be heard filtering down from the bridge and up from the engine room. Red emergency lights came on and they all jumped up and ran toward the bridge only to be stopped by a door that wouldn't open.

"There has to be an override," Max muttered, as he started looking around the edge of the door.

The COMM on the wall beeped. Crash walked over to it, "Crash here."

"Pop off the door's sensor plate," came Eps's voice. "Inside the bottom is a release latch to a long slim panel below. Open that panel and pull down the handle. That will manually release the door and you can pry it open."

"Copy that!"

Max already had the door released by the time Crash had finished talking to Eps. Bear easily manhandled the door open and the four of them spilled out into the corridor, also bathed in red emergency lighting. Standing there was Epsilon surrounded by smoke that was wafting up through the deck hatch.

"Captain! Glad to see you're okay," Crash exclaimed.

"Yes, a very speedy recovery. Most men wouldn't have survived it," said Max.

"Well, it appears that the rumors about Dr. Zubreé are indeed true," Eps said, glancing at Taz. "She's one helluva doctor!"

"I, for one, don't care how you recovered, just that you recovered," Bear said. "I shouldn't have left you."

"Quit killing yourself over this. I gave you an order. You followed it and it all worked out in the end. Now, on to the business at hand. Where's Jess?"

"On the bridge, Captain," Crash answered.

Eps walked back into the mess followed by Max and Crash, who were a little perplexed. He popped the faceplate of the COMM off to reveal a small crank. "The COMMs in the mess, sickbay, engine room and the bridge all have manual generators. Turn the handle a few times fast and it generates enough energy to run it for a few minutes." He cranked it up a few times. "Eps to bridge."

"Bridge, Jess here."

"Sitrep!"

"All systems down, Captain, including life support. Backup power is down too. We're running on emergency batteries, and we're adrift. The alarm board is showing a fire in the engine room. A couple small fires broke out here, but I managed to put them out, though it is a bit smoky right now." The crew suddenly realized how quiet it was. No reassuring rhythmic pulse from the wave drive; no humming of auxiliary systems scattered around the vessel.

"Okay. Max, Bear, Crash: engine room. Get the fire out, get the off-line APU up and running, and figure out what the hell just happened!"

All three responded "Aye" at the same time and headed off to the engine room.

"APU?" Taz asked.

"Auxiliary power unit." Epsilon tried to not let his irritation show. "Let's go, Taz, you're with me. Jess doesn't have a lot of time on the bridge before the air runs out." They started up the ladder to the bridge.

"We can just open the door like we did in the mess, right?" Taz asked, concern evident in her voice. Even though she had only been here a short time, she was pretty adept at summing a person up pretty quickly and she liked Jess. Epsilon, however? The jury was still out on him.

"Not that easy. It's a blast door. Very heavy and can only be opened from the inside. Jess will use up most of the oxygen just manhandling the release. Then we'll need the rest of the guys to help pry it open."

* * *

Eps and Taz arrived at the bridge door and Eps banged on it. "Jess, can you hear me?"

"Yes," came Jess's calm response.

"Can you see any ships or other obstructions out the windows?"

"Negative."

"Taz, head back down to the mess, look out the rear windows carefully and check for anything coming at us."

"On it," she said, as she headed back down the steps.

"Jess," Eps said. "You are going to run out of air. We need to get the bridge's auxiliary life support unit online."

* * *

Max, Bear and Crash pried open the blast door to the engine room and were greeted with a smoldering fire in one of the control cabinets. The automated fire suppression system had kicked in and knocked the fire down. Grabbing a handheld extinguisher, Max put the rest of it out.

"Oh, the captain is NOT going to be happy," Max said, shaking his head. "Okay, Bear, the Auxiliary Power Unit is over there. See the cable looped above it? Plug one end into it and the other end into the receptacle marked 'APU' on the main power grid over there; Crash help me yank these cables out. I'll have to manually patch them together later." The three of them got busy.

\* \* \*

"Captain," Taz said, as she came back up the stairs. "I thought I saw something moving in the distance, but it could have been the stars playing tricks on me."

"If I were a betting man," Eps responded, "my money would be on that you saw something. Which side of the ship?"

"Basically, from behind, maybe a little off to the left."

"Okay, Jess, have you found the ALU under the back console?" There was no answer. "JESS," Eps yelled, louder.

A feeble response came back that Epsilon thought might have been laced with expletives.

"She's suffering from dyspnea, Captain," Taz said. Eps gave her a blank look. "She's not getting enough oxygen, and it is starting to affect her brain. She has slurred speech and isn't making sense. There is no way you can talk her through anything. If we don't get to her soon, she will have permanent brain damage! What about a laser cutter on the door?"

"It would take hours to cut through this door. Damn it!" Eps pounded on the door, frantically looking around, trying to think of something to do to save Jess.

A loud bang came from the engine room along with a soft hum. The lights came back on and Eps could feel the air start to move. "Yes!" Eps hit the sensor panel, the doors opened, and smoke poured out. He ran immediately to Jess, scooped her up, and headed for sickbay.

\* \* \*

Eps had no sooner plopped Jess onto one of the beds in sickbay and Taz was already pushing him out of the way, taking readings, injecting her with an oxygen-rich compound, and putting a high-flow oxygen mask on Jess's face.

Crash bounded into sickbay just as Jess started coughing and came to. "Crash get to the helm. I need to know what's out there," Eps ordered.

"On it," Crash acknowledged and headed to the bridge.

Jess sat up and tried to get out of the bed. "Not so fast, Lieutenant," Taz warned.

"I need to get to the bridge," Jess started. "I thought I saw movement out of the front window right before I blacked out."

Suddenly the klaxon sounded, and Crash's voice came over the COMM. "Captain to the bridge!"

* * *

"What the hell just happened?" Eps exclaimed, as he, an unsteady Jess, and Taz entered the bridge, and he settled into the command chair. Max and Bear were still in the engine room.

On the screen, several weird looking ships started dropping out of hyper drive.

"CONTACT! Bogeys all around us; I count six unidentified vessels surrounding us," Jess barked out, regaining her composure. "Shields up, 100%. Targeting systems still off-line."

"Max, Sitrep!" Eps yelled over the COMM.

"Huh?" Max responded.

"Situation Report Max, what's your status?" Crash barked out.

"Oh," Max said, finally understanding. "Some sort of concentrated proton beam hit us and took out our number one Power Control Unit. All the downstream systems clamped the overload and shut down. I can give you life support, shields, and maneuvering thrusters off the APU."

"I need the main up. I can't outrun them on maneuvering thrusters!"

"I should have main power back in ten minutes. Propulsion systems are down hard. I'll have to reboot them; you should have sub-light in fifteen and wave in twenty minutes."

"Captain lead ship is deploying their forward cannon and locking onto us," Jess said. "We're being hailed."

"On screen."

The image of the forward screen changed to that of the bridge of the opposing vessel. Filling up most of it was a disheveled, bearded man—with a patch over his left eye.

"You've got to be kidding me," Crash mumbled.

"Argh, the infamous Captain Epsilon," the man started. "So, the rumors be true; you DO be havin' *Stingray*."

"Well, sir, you have me at a disadvantage," Eps responded. "And you are?"

"That, Captain, is irrelevant. What IS relevant is that I will take *Stingray* now. Give her up without a fight and I guarantee you and your crew no harm. I will even drop you off at the nearest populated planet."

"Now that is most generous of you, sir. Especially coming from a—pirate," Eps said, motioning toward the eye patch.

"Think it to be—too much?"

"A little over the top," Eps said, nodding. He noticed, out of the corner of his eye, that a very agitated Max had appeared on the bridge. "A counter proposal: you and your band of merry men leave, and I won't blow each and every one of your ships from here to kingdom come."

"Um, Captain?" Max whispered. Eps held his hand up at him. The pirate just roared in laughter, along with his cronies in the background.

"Obviously, Captain, you don't know what kind of weapon I have trained on you," the pirate snorted.

"Oh, I know exactly what it is. It's a Tracor Arms ION cannon, outlawed at the Salada treaty decades ago," Eps responded. The laughing abruptly stopped. Even Max had a stunned look on his face.

"Well, then, you know what it is capable of doing and no

shielding can stop the highly charged and concentrated beam."

"Yup."

"So, then, you will give up *Stingray* without a fight? My previous guarantee still stands," the pirate said, smiling and spreading his hands out in front of him.

"Nope," Eps retorted. "Lieutenant, target the lead vessel!"

"Targeting vessel, aye, Captain," came Jess's quick response as Eps hit a button on his console, severing communications. "Sir, you do realize we don't have targeting and weapons at the moment?"

"Yup. But they don't know that."

"Captain, the ION cannon CAN penetrate the shields," Max shouted.

"Eps, the human body can't survive such a high exposure to the ion radiation," Taz said, extreme distress in her voice.

"We're all gonna be vaporized, Captain!" Bear moaned, nervously. He had just joined the rest of the crew on the bridge after he finished running some cables for Max.

"ION cannon powering up, Captain," Jess said, calmly. She and Crash were the only ones not questioning the Captain's order. They served with him too long to know that he was already three steps ahead of their antagonists. "They're firing!"

Normally when fired upon, the shields would absorb the energy from the attack. In the process, the ship would rock, reacting as if something had slammed into it. In this case, the ION weapon delivered a concentrated beam small enough to slice through the shield. As the beam got its foothold through the shield, it expanded creating a larger and larger hole. As this continued, the shields would eventually collapse leaving the ship vulnerable to the lethal ion radiation, frying any living tissue it encountered. But the ship itself was left intact unless, of course, part of the ship was made from organic material.

"Pirate vessel has stopped firing. Shields holding at 99%," Jess reported matter-of-factly.

"Damage control showing all systems nominal. No damage to *Stingray*," Bear reported, astonished.

"And it appears we are still alive, Captain," Jess said, with just a hint of sarcasm.

"Of course, we're alive," Eps retorted, irritated.

"But how?" Bear asked.

"Captain, pirate vessels are drifting," Jess interrupted. "And I'm no longer picking up life signs aboard any of the vessels. The ION beam must have disrupted our sensors."

"Maneuvering to avoid a collision," Crash said, with the slightest smirk on his face.

"Max, can you hack into their internal COMM?"

"On it," Max said, as he feverishly banged away on his console. "Video on screen now."

On the main screen, the familiar bridge was displayed as before, but this time minus the face of the pirate. "Zoom out," Eps ordered. The image zoomed out to show several charred mounds of goo, smoke rising from each one. A collective gasp was uttered by all on deck. "Max, when can I have my weapons?"

"Right now, Captain," Max said, as be pressed an assortment of buttons. "Main power is back up and engine control systems are still rebooting."

"Very well then," Eps said. "Lieutenant, target the ION cannon and destroy it and her ship."

"Aye, Captain, target acquired and firing," Jess responded. From below the nose of *Stingray* leapt a purple beam of light. It collided with the pirate vessel, which erupted into a massive ball of flame. Minutes later, all that was left was scattered parts and wreckage.

"Scan the other vessels. Any other ION cannons?" Eps asked.

"Scanning," Jess said. "Negative. That was the only one."

"Max, engines?" Eps asked.

"All systems are online. You have full sub-light. Wave drive will be available shortly."

"I expect you will rectify this situation so that it can't happen again?"

"Oh, Captain," Max responded with a faraway look.

"Rectify it I shall." Coming back to this reality, he continued, "But how did you know the ION beam would be absorbed by the shields?"

"Actually, it didn't absorb it. It reflected the energy back out, like a mirror but with an added twist. The shields couldn't absorb this type of energy, so it dispersed it along the entire surface area of the shields and then reflected it outward in all directions. Since the pirate ships' shields couldn't deflect the ion beam, well, you saw the results."

All eyes were on Eps; incredulous stares from everyone. Only Jess had a smirk on her face. "I read the manual," Eps said, with a straight face. After a short pause for effect, he added, "Hey, I had a lot of time on my hands, okay?" Everyone busted up laughing. "Crash, resume our course."

"Aye, Captain," he said, still chuckling. Crash engaged the wave drive, and they were, once again, underway.

"Crash and I will hold down the bridge, the rest of you get some rest," Eps ordered, noticing that Jess was missing. The rest of the crew exited the bridge and headed to their quarters.

* * *

"What the hell is going on out there, Smythe?" Roth bellowed at Jess over the secure COMM. "You broke out a prisoner from Taurus-9! Several guards dead!"

She had slipped unnoticed off the bridge and went to her quarters to report in to Roth. "He's assembling a crew. In order to get Jimmy Zubreé, he had to agree to break out his sister Tamson from Taurus-9."

"What is he up to, Smythe?"

"I don't know. He had me execute a secure program. I'm not sure where we are going, and we just ran into pirates. I almost have him convinced to give *Stingray* back. I just think he is putting his affairs in order."

"Look Smythe, if you want to see your sister alive—"

"Don't threaten me, Roth. I'm keeping my end of the

bargain. You better keep yours. Have to go." She severed communications and buried her head in her hands. She stood up, composed herself, and headed out into the corridor.

* * *

After a couple minutes, Eps asked, "so, buddy, you look relieved to have your sister back?"

"Yes. Very relieved. Thanks, Eps. So—what about you and Jess, eh?" Crash asked, with a smile.

"What about her?"

"No—not 'what about HER?' What about you TWO? You look glad to have HER back."

The noise of a commotion on the deck below echoed through the open bridge hatch and saved Eps from having to answer that question. He got up and headed down to see Bear had pinned Jess to the bulkhead, his pistol under her chin. Bear had been waiting outside Jess's quarters after he heard shouting coming from within and he overheard the latter part of the conversation. When she emerged, he grabbed her and threw her against the bulkhead.

"Bear, SITREP!" Eps barked as he rounded the corner. Max and Taz came out into the corridor. "I caught this traitor giving us up to Roth!" Bear exclaimed. "This isn't about getting her sister back. It's about giving you—us and this ship to the Conglomerate."

Eps met Jess's eyes. He could see the fire in them. "Stand down, Bear."

"Captain, she's been giving Roth a running narration of our mission and position."

"Bear, stand down."

Bear growled and pushed himself back from Jess as he holstered his pistol. Eps stepped between them, preventing Jess from lashing out at Bear.

"I appreciate your diligence, Bear. I ordered Jess to give updates to Roth, feeding him misinformation. My hope was to keep Maggie alive by making Roth think *Stingray* was still within his grasp."

"You should have let us know."

Eps walked up to Bear, got into his face, and stared him in the eye. "I don't have to explain my every move. You have a problem with that, there's the door."

"Dude," Max said to Bear, as he walked up. "Take it easy. We're all cool here."

"No problem, Captain," Bear said. Max pulled his friend away, and they walked into the mess. Taz retreated into sickbay and Crash headed up the ladder to the bridge, leaving Eps and Jess alone in the corridor. Eps stared at her with those cold piercing eyes, showing no emotion.

"Why did you cover for me?" Jess finally asked.

"I would've done the same thing you did."

"How do you know I'm not a traitor?"

"I just know."

Jess looked at the floor. "She's dead, isn't she?"

"Probably," Eps said. He was always a straight shooter and never sugar-coated anything.

Jess started to cry. Eps pulled her to him and enveloped his arms around her. "It's all my fault," she said.

"No, if it's anyone's fault, it's mine. It's me and *Stingray* they're after. You and your family were collateral damage. Damage they don't care about. We're going to bring her back and make those who are responsible for this, pay. You have my word on that."

# CHAPTER SIX

*Stingray* dropped out of wave drive at the edge of an asteroid field. She immediately cloaked herself and raised her shields. "What's going on?" Crash asked no one in particular.

"Not sure," replied Jess. She got up from the command chair and walked over to her station just as Bear relinquished it. "Looks like she's waiting for a further course change."

"That's correct," Epsilon said, as he walked onto the bridge. "Program Zeta326 brought us here. Anybody could come here. But only I know which asteroid is the right one."

"Not true," Jess retorted. "Looks like someone else knows about your asteroid. Second-one in, bearing zero-five degrees. A long-range pleasure craft is docked to the side of the rock. I'm assuming the rock is made of that same material as your moon was, since I'm only getting scattered life signs through the open hatch in the ship."

"I wonder why the alarm didn't trip," Eps muttered. "Crash lay in a course. Bring us around the opposite side of the asteroid."

"Aye, Captain," Crash acknowledged. He expertly threaded *Stingray* through the maze of asteroids to the one with the ship docked to it. As they came around the backside, a small cavern came into view.

"Come about and line up aft with that cavern at a five-degree angle toward starboard."

"She's too big to fit in there."

"Just bring the ass-end of the ship exactly one point two meters from it at a ninety-eight-degree vertical angle, seven-degree starboard angle, and twelve-degree rotation. And please line-up without crashing into it." Eps saw the slightest smirk on Jess's face. Crash didn't show any sign of acknowledging that he heard what Eps said, as he was used to being ribbed about it every so often. During his first deployment on the *Freedom,* he ran her straight into an asteroid. Oh, he got a proper chewing out, by not only Eps but also by the chief engineer. The ironic part was they had just finished an intense battle with several pirate ships. He handled the *Freedom* expertly and avoided several near misses. He supposed that being branded with the nickname "Crash" for the rest of his life was better than being relieved of duties and bumped down a grade, thanks to the Captain. From that moment on, he was one hundred percent loyal to Captain Epsilon; if Eps said to jump off a cliff, he'd jump off a cliff (because he knew Eps would have a plan).

This time he maneuvered *Stingray* with ease and without incident. "Crash hold down the fort. Bear and Max arm up and meet me at the transporter." Eps hit the COMM button. "Eps to Taz."

"Taz here," came her reply. She gave up trying to force Eps into using her given name. She figured the more she tried, the more likely that he'd come up with something worse. Besides, secretly she kind of liked it. It reminded her of a character she saw in a very, very old and retro-animated series while she was in prison.

"Meet me at the transporter. Eps out," he said, as he closed the COMM. "Jess, you're with me." Both of them exited the bridge and headed down to the hangar deck.

\* \* \*

Everyone was assembled in front of the transporter. "Okay," Eps started. "This is one of my supply stashes. It is made from a rock that is impenetrable to sensors. All the asteroids here are made of the same material. There's an airlock hidden in the front. Past the airlock is the main cavern with rows of supplies. There is only one spot in the back of the cavern that you can beam into and the transport pad on the ship has to be aligned precisely, which Crash has already done. We'll beam in and proceed to the airlock. We'll assume the cavern has been compromised. As soon as we materialize, Bear take the right side, Max to the left. Jess and I will go up the middle. Taz, stay behind us." Eps handed everyone goggles. "These are sensor goggles. They will let you see in the dark and are not bothered by light. Sensors will work inside the cavern." Eps grabbed a spare pistol and handed it to Taz.

"No thanks," she responded. "I don't like those things."

"Suit yourself, just stay behind me. Our position will be given away by the transport artifact, so move out as soon as we materialize. Assuming no resistance, we'll rendezvous at the airlock door on the opposite side of the cavern. Let's saddle up, people!" They assembled, weapons at the ready, on the transport platform with Eps and Jess in the middle, Bear to the right, Max to the left, and Taz behind Eps and Jess. They donned and activated their goggles. "Eps to Crash, ready for transport."

"Aye, Captain, transporting now," Crash responded.

The team dematerialized on *Stingray* and rematerialized in the belly of the asteroid. The transport artifact lit up the cavern for a second and then it was pitch black, except for an eerie, red, pulsating glow coming from the other side of the cavern. Their sensor goggles allowed them to see both visually and tactically in the dark cavern. As soon as they were whole again, they all quickly moved out on their pre-planned courses. The sensors showed the cavern devoid of life, only rows and rows of crates containing unknown materials. The team quickly converged on the airlock door. The panel to the right indicated the pressure was normalized on the other side and it was safe to open the door. The red indicator light was blinking brightly, informing all that cared that the alarm had been tripped. The panel on the other side required a retinal scan to gain access. Their sensors showed clear but could only see directly in front of the door due to the rock walls creating severe angles of dead space. Eps motioned to remove the goggles and whispered, "Ready," and he put his eye in front of the retinal sensor. The door slid open and the team burst through the door to find a male and female human completely naked and all tangled up in each other. The two were going at it so feverishly that they didn't hear the sound of the door sliding open over their own moans and guttural sounds. It was an awkward few seconds as the team's brains processed the visual input. That, coupled with the strong smell of sex mixed with sweat, ordered the release of a whole host of hormones into the team's bloodstreams. Since their adrenaline levels were already elevated, it didn't take much to cause certain parts of their bodies to react accordingly. It was another few seconds before the two lovers realized they had an audience; an audience pointing guns at them, but an audience none the less.

She saw them first and screamed.

"Yeah, baby!" he yelled, and became even more aroused since he misinterpreted her scream as her being on the verge of an orgasm. He increased his pelvic thrusts, pushing harder and deeper inside of her. His lean muscular buttocks tightened and flexed with his pulsating rhythm.

"STOP!" she yelled, finally pushing and kicking him off her.

"What the hell is your problem?" he yelled back, as he rolled off her and withdrew from her love hole. Jess was impressed with his physique: bulging biceps, sculpted pecs, washboard abs, muscular defined glutes and legs, and a rock-hard erection. Jess felt a slight tingle in her nether regions causing her to shift her stance. Seeing the terror on his lover's face coupled with the fact that she covered her breasts with her hands and closed her legs tight, he turned around and saw the three men and one woman training their weapons on them. He immediately lost his stature, no longer standing at attention, and instinctively his hand went to his groin to cover his manhood. "Oh shit!"

"Who do you think you are coming here and threatening us?" she barked out. Eps was in the right position to get a full view of this beauty right up the alley before she covered up and closed her legs and he was immediately aroused. She was a curly brunette. Nice, soft-looking breasts that jiggled just slightly off the sides of her chest with pert nipples. She was fit, with sexy, toned arms, toned, muscular legs, and tight abs. Eps saw a green stone in her belly button, right over her glistening, gaping, engorged, love tunnel.

"Who do you think WE are? Seriously?" Eps retorted.

"You guys are going to be in a lot of trouble. I have VERY influential friends in VERY low places. You just turn right around and march back through that door. We'll part ways, and no one gets hurt."

"Wow! This little snot-nose has balls!" Bear said, incredulously. "Can I just do her right now?"

"Obviously, SIR," she continued with as much sarcasm a cornered, naked woman could muster. "You don't know who I am."

"Seriously, Captain. Can I just do the little bitch and then toss her naked, white ass out the airlock?" Bear asked, again.

"Actually," Eps responded, as he straightened up and holstered his weapon, "I know exactly who you are: Marrah Charisma, daughter of Marco, and heir apparent to the Charisma cartel." The guy's jaw dropped, and the color drained out of Marrah's face. "Oh, snap! You didn't know who she was, did you Jensen Bennett? Odd, given that you're the son of the notorious mobster Buck Bennett, and heir apparent to the Bennett syndicate." Now it was Marrah's turn to drop her jaw. "Oh, the DRAMA! So, Marrah, how long has this affair been going on?"

"A year," Marrah said, looking longingly at Jensen. He reciprocated with the same to Marrah.

"And all that time, you two hadn't figured out who each of you were doinkin'?"

"I figured, why ruin the great thing we had going?" Jensen responded. "I think we both knew we weren't really who we told each other we were. It added to the excitement and as you could see, the sex is really incredible." Marrah smiled and nodded.

"And Daddy doesn't know?"

"No," Marrah said, deflated.

"Seriously, Captain. Let me do her and I'll airlock 'em both," Bear pined.

Jensen moved closer to Marrah, attempting to protect her while still covering himself up. They were scared, and it showed. Realization had set in that these people weren't fazed by their crime syndicate families.

"I'd love to be a fly on the wall when you bring him home," Eps laughed. "Right then! Enough drama. No, Bear, I have other plans for these two. Jess keep them covered. Everyone else stand-down." Everyone except Jess secured their weapons. Turning back to his crew, Eps directed, "Bear left aisle, you'll find munitions. Max, next aisle over are parts. Taz, last aisle is medical. Grab what you need and put them where we came in and have Crash bring them back to *Stingray*." Eps was careful with his word selection, as he didn't want to give away that they had transport capability. The three of them took off as Eps turned back to face the naked lovebirds. "Okay, you two get dressed. If they give you any trouble Jess, shoot him and let Bear have a go at her." Marrah's eyes got huge.

"Aye, Captain, with pleasure," Jess responded with a wide grin. Even though they were talking tough, none of this would come to pass. It just wasn't their style.

"I'll be back in a minute," Eps said, as he disappeared into the cavern.

"Some privacy, please," Jensen said, indignantly.

"Don't fret love. You don't have anything to see that's worth writing home about," Jess lied, secretly hoping to get another peek. "Just man-up." The two of them stood, turned around, and started getting dressed. Jess got her peek as Jensen turned, but then fixated on his ass-cheeks instead. *Wow!* He pulled his shorts on, bringing Jess out of her trance. Marrah was still fumbling with her panties when Jess noticed a large, colorful tattoo of what she thought was a bug, in the small of Marrah's back. It had a long skinny body, two pairs of wings, and a bulging head. *Cute, but yuck! Why do attractive people mark themselves up?*

* * *

Max, Bear, and Taz were like kids in a candy store picking out their goodies. All of the supplies had been gathered and beamed back aboard *Stingray*. The team re-assembled inside the airlock. Marrah and Jensen were fully clothed, holding hands, and very indignant. Jess had holstered her weapon. She stood there, arms crossed, daring him to make a move. She so much wanted an excuse to get physical with him.

"My dad—" Marrah started, but Eps cut her off.

"Don't start, Marrah. I'm not concerned with your father."

"Oh my God! You're the one—" All the color drained from her face. She had heard the rumors of a lone rival busting up one of her dad's illicit deals and killing all but two, who got away. One of them was her dad, who was seriously wounded. At that moment, she realized they were cooked.

"You're lucky I don't shoot you both, or worse," Eps said, giving a sideways glance at Bear, who just grinned. "For sparing your lives, here's what you're going to do for me." He handed her a box that contained what looked like an old-fashioned typewriter from Earth. Marrah took it, with a perplexed look on her face. "The two of you will depart here and head straight to the Côte de Mann Resort. You will check into the SkyView Tower in a star-gazer suite. When the Conglomerate ships show up, you will use that device to send me a message. I want you to go down to the Star Lounge and look for this girl," Eps showed them a picture of Maggie. "Go back to your suite and type a message to let me know whether or not they brought her. Understand?"

"The Conglomerate will tag us," Jensen said. "Besides, they'll intercept the COMM and trace it back to our room."

"They're not interested in you. That device creates a secure connection back here, and it's so old-school that they won't even notice. Register under an assumed name. You do it all the time." Eps tossed Jensen a red velvet pouch with a dozen gold coins in it. "Show your lady a good time and finish what we interrupted here.

You two need to work your futures out. Personally, I'd stick to it," he said to both of them.

"How do you know we just won't take off?" Jensen asked.

Eps looked at Bear. Without urging, Bear walked to Marrah and ran his fingers through her hair, grabbed the back of her head and snapped it back. He started to lean toward her face when Jensen stepped closer to him. "Really?" Bear asked, giving him a hard-sideways look. Jensen looked momentarily flustered. Turning back to Marrah, Bear smiled evilly. "I never forget a pretty face."

"We wouldn't skip out on someone paying us to do a job," Marrah said, swallowing hard. "Daddy taught me that would be bad business."

"Smart girl. Now scram!" Eps said. Marrah wrangled out of Bear's hold, who let out a dastardly laugh. Marrah and Jensen quickly disappeared through the hatch, back into their ship, and departed without another word.

* * *

After securing the asteroid, the team returned to *Stingray*.

"Captain," Crash said, as he joined the rest of the crew in the cargo bay. "I took the liberty of re-attaching the sub-space relay on the asteroid. It appeared that something bumped it, and that's why we never received the alarm signal. The system is reset and working perfectly now."

"Thanks," Eps said, as he walked over to a small case sitting atop a large crate. He opened it as he announced, "Everyone gather 'round, please. Since *Stingray* now has as complete a crew as we are going to get, I feel it is necessary to make this official before we go into battle." He took out a set of gold anchors and pinned them to Bear's collar. "By the authority vested in me as Captain of this vessel, I hereby appoint you to the rank of Chief Petty Officer. Congratulations, Chief," Eps said. He shook Bear's hand as everyone applauded. "Are you up for the challenge?"

"Wow! I ain't never been given nothin' by nobody. I can handle anything you throw at me, sir."

"Good! That's what I want to hear," Eps said, as he turned back to the case. He took out a set of double silver bars and pinned them to Max's collar. "By the authority vested in me as Captain of this vessel, I hereby appoint you to the rank of Lieutenant and commission you as Chief Engineer of the vessel *Stingray*. Congratulations Lieutenant," Eps said, shaking his hand.

Max got all teary eyed. "I don't know what to say, Captain. Just that this is such an honor and I won't let you down. I want to thank my mother for nurturing me—"

"I know you won't let me down." Eps said, cutting him off mid-sentence and shaking his hand. He turned back to the box and removed a double silver bar and a silver caduceus. He walked over to Taz and pinned them to her collar. "By the authority vested in me as Captain of this vessel, I hereby appoint you to the rank of Lieutenant and commission you as Chief Medical Officer of *Stingray*. Congratulations, Lieutenant," he said, shaking her hand.

"Gee—thanks," Taz said, somewhat reluctantly and with reticence.

"Don't worry, Captain," Crash said. "It'll grow on her. And you'll grow on her too."

He turned back to the box and removed a set of gold oak leaves. He walked over to Crash and pinned them to his collar. "By the authority vested in me as Captain of this vessel, I hereby appoint you to the rank of Lt. Commander and commission you as Chief Helmsman of *Stingray*. Congratulations Lieutenant Commander," he said, shaking his hand.

"Thank you, sir!" Crash saluted and Eps saluted back.

Eps turned back to the box for a final time. He pulled out a set of silver oak leaves, closed the lid, and pinned them on Jess's collar. "By the authority vested in me as Captain of this vessel, I hereby promote you to the rank of Commander and commission you as Executive Officer of the vessel *Stingray*. Congratulations, Commander," he said, shaking her hand. "This should have been done a long time ago, Jess."

"Thank you, sir!" Jess saluted and Eps saluted back.

"Right, then! As you know, I'm extremely intrigued and

fascinated with Earth history. What is more fitting, then, to use these insignias and ranks that reach so far back to the one planet that is standing alone in the fight with the corrupt and diabolical organization known as the Conglomerate. Today we pay homage to the brave souls who gave their lives, so that many others could live a free life. These insignias and ranks date back to the Navy of the United States of America. Over the centuries, as alliances were made, they looked to the structure of the finest nation on the planet Earth. Even as her individual nations merged into a unified planetary government, her military resembled that of the USA's. As Earth influenced alliances, they quickly adopted Earth's military and government structure. I am reminded of the quote: 'Government of the people, by the people, for the people' by Abraham Lincoln, the sixteenth President of the United States, some two millennia ago. Lest we not forget this hallmark philosophy. Another quote by that same good president: 'America will never be destroyed from the outside. If we falter and lose our freedoms, it will be because we destroyed ourselves.' America did just that at one point, but fortunately, she recovered in time. History has repeated itself, just recently, with the fall of the Planetary Alliance. But starting today, we too can recover."

Even with the hum of the engines in the cavernous cargo bay, you could hear a pin drop. "Enough with blowing smoke up your collective butts. Stations everyone!"

As the new crew of *Stingray* headed topside, Eps felt rejuvenated. He was back in the saddle and it felt great!

* * *

*Stingray's* crew assembled on the bridge. "Course to Prison-12 laid in Captain, shall I engage?" Crash asked.

"Negative," Eps replied. "I never thought I would say this, but Commander, get me Admiral Roth on the COMM"

"Aye, sir," Jess said, as she established the link.

The image of the back of Roth's head materialized on the screen. "A video link is a little bold of you, Smythe," Roth chastised, as he turned to face his screen. "Oh, Captain Epsilon. Well then, I guess it's best that this charade comes to an end. Give me *Stingray* back NOW!"

"Okay, Roth," Eps said.

"That's ADMIRAL Roth to you, Epsilon—did you say 'okay'?"

"You're not deserving of the rank of admiral, Roth. And yes, I said 'okay'. You can have *Stingray* back with the following conditions: One, you will bring Maggie, unharmed, to the Star Lounge at the Côte de Mann Resort in two days' time. I will exchange *Stingray* for her just as you originally agreed to do with Jessie."

"You are NOT in a position to make any conditions, Epsilon," Roth said, cutting Eps off and starting to turn red in the face.

"Actually, ADMIRAL," Eps countered as he stood up. "I'm in a very good position to make demands as I don't think you can produce Maggie. I, unfortunately, believe she is already dead." Eps detected the slightest wince from Jess. "Two, I want Jessie Smythe promoted to the rank of Commander and given an honorable discharge. Three, all charges against me and any of my crew are dropped with no new charges brought. And finally, you allow us safe passage in one of *Stingray*'s shuttles away from the resort. You agree to that, you can have her back."

Roth glared long and hard at Eps. "Fine—two days—Côte de Mann Resort." Roth terminated the link.

Silence enveloped the bridge, only the electronics emitted any noise. "You can't give him *Stingray*," Taz implored, finally breaking the silence.

"He's not gonna," Bear said. "Roth can't deliver on those promises, can he Captain?"

"No, he can't, Bear. No, he can't," Eps replied. He sat back down and pressed some buttons. A portly fellow appeared on the screen. He had brown hair, a mustache, and a very tan complexion. "Hello Marco."

"Epsilon? Is that you? I heard you were dead," Marco

answered.

"Well, obviously, I'm not. I need a favor."

"I don't owe you anything, Epsilon, especially after that fiasco."

"Yes, you do owe me. You didn't forget that you survived that bloodbath, did you?"

"Grrr."

"Besides, I have Marrah."

"WHAT? You wouldn't!" Marco's face turned purple. "That's low, even for you, Epsilon."

"Oh, simmer down, Marco. You're going to pop a blood vessel. I caught her and her boyfriend doing the wild thing on one of my—um—properties. You're lucky I didn't shoot them on sight."

"Was she with that Bennett kid?"

"Yup."

"Well, you have my permission to shoot HIM. I'll deal with her."

"Marco, I think you and Buck need to face the facts. One day, those kids are going to take over the family businesses. Might not be a bad thing if they are on more than speaking terms. Especially when their respective fathers aren't."

Marco sighed. "We're dinosaurs, eh, Epsilon?"

"Dinosaurs we are, Marco, more than you realize. I sent the two lovebirds off to the Côte de Mann Resort for a long romantic weekend on me."

"I don't expect that it's a coincidence that the Conglomerate just dispatched the Fifth Fleet there, is it?"

"Nope. Don't worry; they aren't going to be in harm's way. I just need a little on-scene intel."

"What do you need from me?"

"I need you to poll your contacts at Prison-12 to see if a certain person is still there and to let me know if, or when, they are moved off planet."

"Maggie Smythe?"

"Yes."

"Foul situation. I assume her sister is with you?"

"Yes."

"She is indeed in Prison-12. When I saw the name, I took an interest. Thought about breaking her out, but even I don't have those kinds of resources." Marco was looking off screen and punching some keys while he was talking. "Nope. No orders to move her."

"How solid is your source?"

"Rock solid. You're going after her, aren't you?"

"Yes."

Marco let out a low whistle. "You always had balls, Epsilon. I'll give you that and wish you luck, my old friend. I'll let you know if they move her. And thanks for not vaporizing my kid. She can be a royal pain-in-the-ass at times, but she's a good kid." Marco severed the COMM.

"Crash, execute course to Prison-12, flank speed."

"Aye, Captain, course executing," Crash confirmed. *Stingray* spooled up to maximum wave, running at one hundred percent on the positron generator. "We should be there in just under twenty-four hours."

"Right, everyone head to quarters and get some rest. We'll meet in the mess in twelve hours and go over our rescue plan," Eps ordered.

After everyone filed out Jess said, "Eps, I don't have a plan."

He put his hands on her shoulders, squeezed, and said, "Jess, we'll figure it out."

## CHAPTER SEVEN

Epsilon was lying on his bed, drifting in and out of a restless sleep. He knew the odds of a successful outcome to this mission were slim. But he had no choice. He had to rescue Maggie or avenge her death. He just hoped that none of his crew was killed in the process.

"Captain," Bear's voice came over the COMM.

Eps hit a button on the COMM unit next to his bed and responded, "Eps here."

"Incoming encrypted message from Marrah, sir."

"Send it to my screen." On his screen the following message appeared:

```
BEGIN    TRANSMISSION    ARRIVED    AT
TARGET AS INSTRUCTED STOP NO ENEMY
VESSELS  STOP  QUICK  LOOK  THROUGH
LOUNGE  NO  JOY  STOP  WILL  REPORT
AGAIN STOP END
```

Epsilon had to chuckle; the lovebirds were certainly getting into their cloak and dagger role. He could imagine the passion they would have after all this role playing was over with. Eps typed back:

```
ACKNOWLEDGED STOP KEEP ME APPRISED
END TRANSMISSION
```

Epsilon laid back down and drifted off to sleep.

* * *

"Captain," Jess said, over the COMM, waking Epsilon from the deep sleep that he had finally found.

"Eps, here," he replied, a little groggy.

"Need you on the bridge ASAP, sir."

"Copy. On my way." Eps dressed quickly and ran up the flight of stairs and entered the bridge. "SITREP!"

"Captain," Jess started, as she relinquished the command chair and returned to her tactical station. "Several high-speed contacts to port on an intercept course. These guys are really fast, sir."

"Conglomerate?" Eps asked, as he sat down in his chair.

"Negative, they aren't squawking and they're way too fast for Conglomerate warships."

"On screen."

Jess fiddled with the controls, and a small, blurry image appeared on the screen. "That's the best I can get, Captain. They are still at the extreme range of our sensors," she said.

"Hmm," Eps mused. "There is something strangely familiar about that ship." Suddenly the image got bigger and clearer. Four large, identical, and unidentified vessels flying in tight formation appeared. The core of the ship was fat, round, and long. The ship itself had the color of evergreen with black bands that had short spike-looking things protruding out. The alternate bands glowed an iridescent green. What appeared to be wings were attached to the top, about halfway down. On top of the front edge sat an oblong structure, which Eps assumed was their bridge, while a shaft stuck out of the rear of the ship.

"Whoa," Jess exclaimed. "Damn, they're fast! They're on a parallel course now, sir. Should be off our port bow in a matter of minutes."

"Well, I'll be," Eps remarked, with a smile on his face.

"They look like fat honeybees," Crash observed. Breeding honeybees became a lucrative business throughout the Alliance. The demand for honey, a sweet substance only found on Earth, skyrocketed and breeders popped up all over Alliance planets.

The klaxon sounded, and the automated "Intruder Alert, Bridge" sounded over the ship-wide COMM. The bridge was enveloped in the bright light of the transport artifact. Before it was finished, Jess was on her feet, weapon drawn and trained on three beings that materialized on *Stingray's* bridge. Within seconds, Bear was on the bridge, laser rifle aimed on the intruders. Max was only a few steps behind him, rifle in hand.

The intruders were tall, with the one in the middle being the tallest. They were attired in what appeared to be dark green military uniforms that complemented their bright green skin. Even not knowing the insignias, it really wasn't difficult to figure out the middle one was the commanding officer; it had more insignias and medals on its "chest". They had triangular shaped heads, with one of the points facing forward that made up their nose and mouth. The bulging eyes were located at the back points on either side, having the same green color as their bodies. Two antennae protruded out from in-between their eyes. The sight was somewhat unnerving. The body, holding up the head, was really nothing more than a stalk or shaft that terminated at a large, scaly, elongated bulb. A third of the way down the stalk were two arms, one on each side. The arms were thick and had two joints. The second section of the arm was even thicker than the first, with sharp nubs protruding out from the bottom. The final section was about the same thickness as the first section, but also had sharp nubs protruding out from the bottom and ending in a pointed, razor-sharp hook. It looked like the last two sections could act as a reverse claw, easily crushing whatever it grabbed.

Where the stalk turned into the bulb, two green leafy looking wings laid on top. At the same juncture, two skinny legs came out, one on each side. Each leg had four joints and terminated with a foot (that really looked like a bone with several nubs protruding out of each side). The rear set of legs were attached about a third of the way down the bulb.

Epsilon swiveled his chair around to face the intruders. He and Crash were the only ones seated and NOT brandishing a weapon. The two outside beings had drawn their weapons as well. Eps slowly rose. "Well, Captain Rhys! It has been a long time."

"That's Admiral Rhys to you, HUMAN!" the one on the left said.

"Admiral?" Eps returned. "Congratulations on your promotion. They couldn't have promoted a finer officer." Eps approached the admiral, hand extended. The admiral grasped his hand in his claw ever so gingerly, not wanting to crush Eps's hand.

"It is good to see you too, Captain Epsilon, my old friend," Rhys said, with what looked to be an awkward smile on his face. They shook hands and embraced. It was a rather awkward sight to see. "Permission to come aboard, Captain?"

"Permission granted," Eps replied. "Stand-down everyone."

"Pfft," the one on the left of Rhys let out.

Rhys turned to him. "This is my ship's captain, Captain Tordl. He doesn't like humans too much," Rhys laughed.

"I would have never guessed," Eps said, nodding to Tordl who didn't return the nod. Jess, Max and Bear hesitantly lowered their weapons, while the other two intruders held theirs steady.

"Stand-down," Rhys said. They holstered their weapons also. Turning to his left, he continued, "This is my chief of staff, Colonel Uka." Both Uka and Eps exchanged nods.

"Admiral, this is my XO, Commander Smythe. That's Crash, my pilot; Max is Chief Engineer; and Bear is, well, Bear. And this is Dr. Zubreé, our ship's physician." Taz had just walked up on deck to see what all the commotion was about. Turning to his crew, "This is Admiral Rhys, we met many years ago. They belong to a highly advanced race called the Tenoderites who live deep in the frontier."

"Admiral," Max asked. "How did you beam over here while we are in hyper-space? That is just not possible."

"As your captain said, we are HIGHLY advanced, HUMAN!" Tordl responded with as much disdain as he could muster.

"Captain Tordl," Uka cautioned, "If it wasn't for Captain Epsilon, you and I just might not be standing here enjoying our freedom and our 'highly advanced' lifestyle."

"Hrmph," Tordl croaked out.

"Whether you like it or not, the good captain here is part of our history; if not legendary."

"Legendary?" Bear asked.

"Oh yes," Uka replied. "It was," he paused, looking at Eps and choosing his words carefully, "many, many years ago. I was first officer under then, Captain Rhys. An Alliance warship ventured deep into the Frontier and engaged us, totally without provocation."

"That's not possible," Jess said, cutting him off. "The Alliance didn't just go around blasting unknown ships."

"No, as a rule they didn't," Uka continued. "However, this ship was a prototype with a new type of weapon. A prototype to this one." He waved his claws in a circular motion. "Our intelligence service later confirmed a rogue faction of the Alliance was heavily involved in secret weapons research and clandestine operations. They were responsible for the attack. They were ruthlessly testing the new prototype at the expense of any unfortunate vessel to cross its path. At the time, we didn't know it was an Alliance vessel."

"He's right," Eps confirmed. "That branch was later responsible for the fall of the Alliance and the rise of the Conglomerate. They had the financial and political backing of the same corporations that today, make up the Conglomerate. The Alliance was literally caught with its pants down."

"Anyway, it was a hellacious firefight. Of COURSE, we destroyed the Alliance vessel, but not before taking very heavy damage and a large number of casualties. During the skirmish, we detected them sending a subspace message and feared they were requesting reinforcements. We blasted their COMM array before they could complete the transmission...."

\* \* \*

"Captain, picking up a faint, garbled signal, originating deep in the Frontier," said the AWS *Freedom's* communications officer, Lt. Potter.

"What does it say?" Eps asked.

"Can't make it out, sir. It's too weak, and the signal has decayed too much. If we were closer, maybe."

"Hmm. Spurious noise?"

"Not sure, sir."

"Opinion, Lieutenant?"

"My gut says it's a distress signal from an Alliance vessel, but it can't be because no Alliance vessels venture that deep into the Frontier."

\* \* \*

"As we were making repairs and tending to the injured, another vessel approached, one that we knew was Alliance," Uka continued.

\* \* \*

"Captain, unidentified vessel. Looks like she has taken heavy damage and is adrift. Huge debris field, total destruction of another vessel," said Commander Puck, the *Freedom's* XO.

"Alliance?" Eps asked.

"Don't think so, sir."

"Long range scans?"

"Clear sir, but our scanners aren't picking up this vessel in front of us, except at close range and only because she's damaged."

"Battle Stations!" Eps ordered. The klaxon sounded, and the bridge lights switched to red.

"Battle stations! All hands man your battle stations! This is not a drill!" Lt. Potter's voice bellowed from the ship-wide COMM.

"Try hailing them, Lieutenant."

"Aye, sir, hailing now. No response. Their COMM array is totally destroyed."

"Life signs, commander?"

"Sensors show multiple unidentified life forms, sir," Puck responded. "And a lot of dead signs also. However, the atmosphere inside is Oxygen/Nitrogen; it's breathable."

"Prepare a shuttle. I want a security and medical detail."

\* \* \*

It took two tries, but the boarding party finally found an intact docking port. When the door slid open, they were greeted by a half dozen bloodied Tenoderites pointing rifles at them. Eps stepped through the door, hands up, and said, "Do you speak English?"

"Yes, I am Rhys, captain of this vessel," Rhys said.

"I am Epsilon, captain of the Planetary Alliance vessel *Freedom*. We are here to help."

\* \* \*

"To sum it up," Rhys said, taking over the story, "Captain Epsilon and the crew of the *Freedom* helped us tend to the wounded and get our ship repaired enough to make a run for our home world. We wondered for years why the Alliance never made another attempt to engage us or came looking for us. We later encountered an Alliance merchant vessel in distress. It had navigational problems and ventured off course and into our territory. By the time we found it, there was only one man barely alive. The life support systems gave out days before. The rest of the crew had abandoned ship in a shuttle, but it exploded as it separated from the cargo ship. I recognized this man from our encounter with the *Freedom*. He said that Captain Epsilon ordered every crew member to never speak of their encounter with us and that the Captain had heard rumblings of a supersecret agency developing high-tech weaponry that had been funded by unknown parties. They all agreed that for the survival of our race, they would all take the knowledge of our existence to their graves." Rhys turned to Jess, "That, my dear, shows how much respect your captain commands."

"So, Captain," Jess started with a smile, "you never logged the incident?"

"No," Eps retorted, as seriously as he could. "I logged the incident as I saw it: We responded to an unknown transmission that my COMM officer felt was a distress signal. We arrived at the source location, found a large debris field of an unknown matter, no bodies, no transmission, no planets, or other vessels nearby. We lingered for a day or so to sweep the area, found nothing, and returned to Alliance space."

"Hrmph," Bear said.

"Well, Admiral, you didn't come all this way to give us humans a history lesson, did you?" Eps said.

"No," Rhys responded. "We sure didn't. We have reason to believe you are on a mission to rescue a certain young lady who is near and dear to you, from a most dreadful place: Prison-12."

"As a matter of fact, we are. Would you like to give us a hand? Additional firepower couldn't hurt."

"Yes, we would. In addition to extra firepower, I have two platoons of marines at your disposal."

There was dead silence on the bridge. That wasn't the response that any of *Stingray's* crew was expecting.

Jess was the first to break the silence. "Why?"

"Quite simple, Commander," Rhys answered. "Prison-12 also houses one of our own: Prince Papu, heir to the throne. The

Prince decided to vacation on one of our remote, rugged planets, close to Conglomerate space. Trying to avoid the scrutiny of our overzealous press corps, he covertly snuck out with a minimal security detail. Upon arriving, they were surprised and overpowered by Conglomerate Marines, holding some sort of training exercise. He was the only one of our kind that survived the firefight. By the time our reinforcements arrived, they were gone. We surmised he would be taken to Prison-12 until they could determine what species he was. Two weeks ago, it was confirmed.

"Our intelligence also indicates that he is in the same ward as Maggie is in. Since the Conglomerate has no knowledge of our species, thanks to your captain, they aren't too interested in him at the moment. Consider this as payback for a favor many, many moons ago."

"Payback with a bonus," Bear muttered.

"Bonus or not, this will greatly increase chances of a successful mission outcome," Eps said. "We'll take you up on your offer."

"Excellent. You can brief the Colonel on your rescue plan, and he will assist with integrating us into it. Tordl and I will return to our ship."

"It was good seeing you again, Rhys."

"Likewise, Epsilon, likewise." Rhys pushed a button on his wristband and the two of them disappeared into the transport artifact.

* * *

Crash set *Stingray* on full autopilot and joined the rest of the crew, along with Colonel Uka, in the mess. In full auto mode, *Stingray* would use her extensive artificial intelligence routines to monitor and respond to any situation that could arise, expected or unexpected. Additionally, he routed the status updates to the monitor in the mess.

"Okay. Bear has come up with a plan to get into Prison-12," Eps said. "Once inside, we will have to play it by ear."

"'Play it by ear', Captain?" Uka asked.

"Sorry, it means improvise as we go."

"Ah, the nuance of your primitive language still escapes me."

"So," Bear started. "The prison is located on the planet Camamu. Most of Camamu is rainforest. Her inhabitants are humans who live in pre-industrial era villages with simple, electoral governance. The prison complex is a hub and spoke design. The central spherical building houses the inmates. Deep underneath is where the 'special' inmates are housed. This is where Maggie and Prince Papu are being held. Circling inside the main building is a secure corridor that connects all four spokes. This allows prison personnel to freely move between the spokes and into the remote pods off each spoke. One pod is the guards' quarters; another pod is the COMM center; the third is the shield generator; the last one is the power generator.

"The prison complex itself is surrounded by a state-of-the-art force field and sits in the middle of a barren plain that is two klicks in radius. There is no penetrating the shields like we did on Taurus-9. The planet is so fertile that the guards must mow the plain daily. Otherwise, the jungle will reclaim the land in a matter of a couple of days, reducing their security. However, in order to mow the plain, they have to drive out a huge mechanical, treaded tractor that has a massive laser beam mounted to the front at ground level. They point the beam toward the jungle and drive it all around the prison, vaporizing any vegetation growing. It moves so slowly that it takes four hours to circle the prison complex."

"Why do they use a crawler instead of a flying platform?" Uka speculated. "It would be much more efficient."

"Yes, it would, however, the shields are designed such that if any ship generating a sub-light or anti-gravity field comes within a half-klick of it, the shield strikes it. But you could walk or drive a vehicle right up to it and it wouldn't bother you in the least."

"We heard that the Conglomerate was working on a pre-emptive shield, but we weren't aware they were using it."

"It's not ready for general use. It takes a lot of power to run it, more than a ship is capable of generating for a sustained period of time. Anyway, in order to get this massive crawler out of its garage, they have to create a hole in the shield. Actually, it looks more like the shape of a slice of a pie, with the point starting at the apogee of the shield dome and extending down. They open this 'door' in the shield when the crawler comes out and again when it goes back in. It takes the crawler a full fifteen minutes to come out or go in, and during that time, the 'door' is left open. That is more than enough time to get both of *Stingray's* shuttles and two Tenoderite hornets, all cloaked, inside the shield dome."

"I thought you said a ship can't come within a half-klick of the shield without being vaporized," Crash clarified.

"Yes, I did. However, when they open the 'door', if we line up in single file, perfectly perpendicular to the middle of the opening, we can zip right in without the shield responding to our presence."

"But even cloaked, as we approach the edge of the shield, it will detect the faint field around our ships," Uka said. "I've seen the specs on it and it is just that sensitive."

"Yes, but the sides of the opening are deadened; otherwise an opening can't be made. That is why, right before the crawler exits, two laser tanks are positioned in a combat formation, to deter any attempt of an attack."

"They may not see us or pick us up on sensors, but they certainly will hear us coming in using planetary thruster drives," Crash contested.

"We come in on minimal sub-light, with a three-second separation. Yes, it will be tricky to get lined up and once inside, they will hear us when the thrusters engage. First shuttle in, goes long and to the right and takes out the COMM pod; second shuttle in, goes long and to the left and takes out the guards' pod; first hornet in, goes short, loops to the right and takes out the shield generator pod; last hornet in, goes short, loops to the left and takes out the power generation pod."

"Our hornet pilots can handle it, no problem," Uka said, with confidence.

"At the same time, one of the Tenoderite cruisers will destroy all the COMM and surveillance satellites in orbit." Bear looked around. Everyone was nodding in agreement. "There's one other wrinkle: a remote communication facility located deep in the jungle. It is camouflaged so well; you can't detect it with sensors from orbit. It is not protected by a shield for just that reason. Once all hell breaks loose at the complex, the communications tech in that facility will broadcast a mayday to CMC. I have a general idea where it is, but Crash, you will have to scan the area for the transmission, immediately jam it, and then destroy the facility."

Crash nodded.

"Smythe, Taz, and I will be on the first shuttle," Eps took over. "Max and Bear on shuttle two. Once we have destroyed our pods, we'll put down and use *Stingray's* transporter to beam the five of us into the special prisoners' section. The remaining two hornets will provide air cover, being joined by additional hornets. Colonel, you'll beam a contingent of your marines into that same sector at the same time we beam." The colonel nodded. "We'll secure Maggie and the prince and beam them to their respective ships."

"What about the other prisoners?" Uka inquired.

"Do you have the manpower to sweep the prison and secure them? You will also have to detain what guards are in the inmate section."

"Consider it handled, Captain. Though, I don't think the guards will be too keen on being 'detained'."

"Well, do what you have to do."

"How do we know the prisoners aren't there for being really bad?" Taz piped up.

"Since Prince Papu has been there, our intelligence agency has gone to great lengths analyzing how best to rescue him with as little exposure as possible. In doing so, they are confident all the prisoners are there for political reasons; mainly for disagreeing with the Conglomerate. There are no hard 'criminals' housed there, as far as we can tell. That's also how we got wind of your operation and the King immediately authorized me to rendezvous with you to offer our help."

"One more thing," Eps added. "Once the prison has been cleared, I want it destroyed."

"With pleasure, Captain," Bear said, with the biggest smile on his face. He was ecstatic he was going to be able to blow big things up.

* * *

With the briefing over and being energized with a confidence that comes with having a plan, Colonel Uka took his leave, politely declining an invitation to dinner. The crew of *Stingray* sat down to their meal, not realizing until that moment how hungry they really were. Eps looked at his watch.

"Hot date, there, Eps?" Crash teased, grinning, and giving a quick look to Jess. As if on cue, the status monitor beeped with an incoming message.

"Mind getting that Crash?" Eps asked, with a smirk.

Crash got up and hit a button. "Encrypted message from Marrah. Putting it on screen."

```
BEGIN TRANSMISSION 8 CMC CRUISERS
ARRIVED   STOP   LOBBY   AND   LOUNGE
TEAMING  WITH  SECURITY  FORCES  STOP
MARINES  FORMED  A  PERIMETER  AROUND
RESORT  STOP  NO  SIGN  OF  THE  SUBJECT
STOP  AWAITING  FURTHER  ORDERS  END
```

Eps got up and walked over to the monitor and typed in:

```
STAND BY END
```

After he pushed a few buttons, an image of Admiral Roth came on the screen. "Hello Roth, I'm touched; eight cruisers for little ol' me."

"Quit screwing around, Epsilon! Give me *Stingray* now!" Roth exploded.

"We had a deal, Roth. I don't see Maggie in the lounge as agreed."

Roth looked perplexed. He could tell Epsilon was transmitting from *Stingray* by the background. "She's in the lounge," he stammered.

"I don't see her."

"You're on your ship! Of course, you don't see her." Roth was getting really agitated.

"I have eyes in the lounge, and I don't see her." Eps remained calm and cool, no doubt fueling Roth's anxiety.

Roth hesitated for a fraction of a second before replying, "She's sitting in the booth, in the corner by the kitchen doors. She's wearing a red wig and there are three marines with her, who have orders to kill her if you try anything."

"Standby." Eps put the call on hold and typed on the encrypted workspace:

```
CHECK FOR REDHEAD GIRL WITH 3 MEN
IN CORNER BOOTH BY KITCHEN DOOR
END
```

A few seconds later, the screen displayed:

```
STANDBY END
```

Eps pushed some more buttons and Marco Charisma's face appeared. "Hello Marco."

"Eps, thank goodness," Marco replied. "The VidiNet is teeming with reports that the Conglomerate has surrounded the Côte de Mann Resort. The reporters are being stonewalled by the CMC. My sources in the area have gone dark. If Marrah gets hurt in any way, I'm holding you personally responsible, Epsilon!"

"Chill out, Marco. I'm in communication with her as we speak. She's fine."

"What? How?"

"Never mind that. Have they moved Maggie?"

"No."

"Are you sure?"

"Absolutely. No vessel has come or gone from Cammamu in the last five days."

"Thanks for your help, Marco. This will all be over soon and Marrah will be just fine." He severed communications, just as the encrypted screen came up and displayed:

```
RED  HEAD  CONFIRMED  STOP  NOT  SURE
IT'S   THE   TARGET   STOP   AWAITING
FURTHER ORDERS END
```

Epsilon typed on the screen:
```
YOUR     SERVICES     ARE     NO     LONGER
REQUIRED STOP ENJOY YOUR STAY STOP
THIS DEVICE WILL SELF DESTRUCT IN
15 SECONDS  STOP  STAND  BACK  STOP
AND CALL YOUR FATHER WHEN YOU GET
BACK END TRANSMISSION
```

Eps re-activated the screen that Roth was on. "Okay, we confirmed Maggie is in the lounge," Eps said, calling Roth's bluff. "We'll be there in an hour. No funny business, Roth."

"No funny business, Epsilon," Roth warned. Calmness came over him. "It will go down, just as you requested, so long as you give me *Stingray*".

Eps severed the communications. The mess hall fell silent.

Taz was the first one to break the silence. "He's so full of shit, Eps." Everyone chuckled at the vulgarity coming out of such a pretty little mouth.

"You've had a penchant today, doctor," Eps quipped, while smiling at her, "to state the obvious."

## CHAPTER EIGHT

Thirty minutes later, *Stingray* and the Tenoderite cruisers dropped out of hyper-space, immediately cloaked, and assumed a high orbit around Cammamu. "SITREP!" Epsilon barked, as he settled into the command chair.

"Ship is in combat mode," Jess responded, as she vacated the command chair and assumed her station. "Tenoderite cruisers are reporting to Battle Stations. Six squadrons of Hornets are ready for launch, and four platoons of marines are ready for beaming, Captain. I'm detecting a large heat signature inside the complex's shield. I believe they're firing up the crawler, sir."

"Very well. Crash hold down the fort. As soon as you detect the remote facility transmitting, jam the transmission and destroy the facility."

"Aye, Captain," Crash responded.

"Everyone else, let's saddle up!"

* * *

Eps, Jess, and Taz were strapped into their seats in the first shuttle. Bear and Max were, likewise, situated in the second shuttle. Both shuttles departed *Stingray's* hangar bay, rendezvoused with two Hornets, and were sitting cloaked in an active, geosynchronous orbit. When an object orbiting around a planet is observed from the ground and appears to be hovering motionless in the sky, it is referred to as being in a geosynchronous orbit. Normally, this orbit only occurs around the planet's equator. Since the shuttles' engines are capable of propelling the ship in three dimensions simultaneously (a requirement of any faster-than-light vessel), the shuttles are able to defy the gravitational pull, thereby *actively* maintaining a geosynchronous orbit at any point around the globe, not just at the equator. Hence the term: *active geosynchronous orbit*. Another benefit of this orbit is re-entry. Once the shuttles decide to head for the surface, maintaining this orbital position during descent, avoids the majority of atmospheric friction. Whatever little friction does occur, the shields will absorb it and, therefore, no "fireball" surrounds the shuttle. It can't be seen or detected through heat sensors from the surface, which is especially nice if the ship is cloaked to begin with.

They were precisely thirty-five thousand, seven hundred, eighty-six kilometers above and four hundred kilometers due east, of the prison complex, waiting for the opening in the shield to occur. Taz was fidgeting in her seat, bouncing her left leg up and down with her foot. "Relax, Taz," Eps said, tersely.

"I'm not nervous," Taz replied, indignant.

"Could've fooled me."

"I have to pee, all right?"

"Should've thought about that before we left *Stingray*."

"Yeah, well...."

"Okay, here we go," Crash said over the COMM. "Crawler is exiting its garage and approaching the shield."

"I have a lock on it," Jess said, looking at her console. "Shield is opening."

"Roger that," Max responded over the COMM. "Locked on."

"Max, Hornets," Eps spoke into the COMM, "form up on us. Crash, inform Colonel Uka that we are a 'go'."

"Roger that," Crash affirmed.

"Okay, Commander," Eps ordered, "take us in."

"Aye, Captain," Jess responded, as she worked the controls. The shuttle descended straight down to a point about four hundred klicks east of the complex. The second shuttle and the two hornets formed a single-file line directly behind them. When the shuttle was about five hundred meters above the surface, Jess executed a ninety-degree turn to the west, aiming directly for the invisible opening in the shield that the crawler just started through. The inertial dampeners absorbed ninety-nine percent of the G-forces, leaving the crew unaffected by the hellacious turn Jess just made.

Even at minimal sub-light speed, they were inside the shield in the blink of an eye. Engaging the thrusters, the shuttle came to a screeching halt in front of the communications pod and she de-cloaked. Eps wasted no time opening fire on the pod. It erupted in a huge ball of fire. Three seconds later, as they were landing on the ground, the guard pod exploded. Eps could see bodies being launched into the air, vaporizing as they hit the shield. As the second shuttle was setting down next to them, the shield generator pod blew up with such force that the shuttle lurched. If they hadn't remained strapped in, all three of them would have been thrown to the opposite side of the craft. The last hornet now arrived and leveled the power generator pod, rendering the complex dark, with only emergency battery backups powering essential systems. Looking up, Epsilon saw three momentary bright flashes in the sky. The communication and surveillance satellites had just been vaporized by one of the Tenoderite cruisers. It was followed by a purple streak of light that flew across the sky and impacted the ground a distance away, resulting in a spectacular fireball.

The events took place with such speed and precision, the operators of the two tanks outside didn't have time to comprehend the attack and react before three additional hornets swooped in and blew up the tanks and the crawler. "Captain and Max," Crash said over the COMM. "Standby for teams' transport."

The crew quickly unstrapped. Eps and Jess grabbed laser rifles off the rack. Taz, now even more nervous, grabbed a spare holster, strapped it on and secured a Kramer-2 in it. "Yes, I know how to use it, even though I prefer not to have to," Taz answered Eps's unasked question. "I'm actually a pretty good shot," Taz beamed.

"Okay," Eps said. "Crash, ready for transport."

* * *

Eps, Jess, and Taz materialized inside a large, dimly lit, very long hallway. Each side of the hall was lined with cells that had thick, steel bars as doors. Each cell was occupied with one or two beings, looking out, wondering what was going on. Red lights were eerily pulsating, and the klaxon went silent shortly after they materialized. In the middle of the room were several guards in an obvious panic. Eps and Jess leveled their rifles at them.

"Freeze!" Eps ordered. "Drop your weapons!" A transport artifact off to Epsilon's right lit up the room as Max and Bear materialized. They quickly drew a bead on the guards. Another transport artifact behind Eps lit the room up again and a dozen armed Tenoderite marines materialized. Realizing they were outgunned, the guards dropped their weapons and surrendered.

Max and Bear made quick time of tying the guards up. They positioned them in a circle, all facing out, with their wrists bound behind their backs and to each other's wrists.

"Didn't expect to see you here, Colonel," Eps said.

"I wouldn't have missed it for the world," Uka said, smiling.

Eps recognized one of the "guards" as the warden and walked up to him. "Warden."

"Epsilon," the warden replied.

"You have one of their kind." Eps motioned in the direction of the Tenoderites. "Where is he?" The warden remained silent and defiant. "Suit yourself." Eps turned to one of the Tenoderite marines and motioned for him to come over. Eps took the marine's free claw and held it up. "I've seen what one of these can do to human flesh and bone. I suggest somebody starts talking real quick."

"First cell on the right," one of the guards volunteered, nodding toward one end of the hall. The marine whose claw Eps was holding pulled it back. He and three other marines double-timed it to the cell.

"Colonel," the marine said, "The Prince is in here. Stand back, Your Highness." The marine blasted the door and using his claws bent it obscenely on its hinges. Prince Papu was helped from the cell and brought to the rest of the Tenoderites.

"Captain," Uka said, "We will take the Prince back to our ship for medical treatment."

"No," said Papu, weakly. "We must free the rest of these beings. They are being held...." His voice trailed off. The two marines who were propping up the Prince tightened their hold on him to prevent him from falling to the floor.

"Your Highness, we already have a plan underway to liberate the prison. I must insist we get you back to our ship. Captain, my marines are at your disposal. Thank you."

"No," Eps said, "Thank YOU." The transport artifact took the Prince, Uka, and the two marines, leaving the remaining ten marines.

"Now it's my turn," Jess said, as she walked up to the warden. "Where's my sister?" The warden just sneered at her. Eps watched a coldness creep over Jess and felt the hair on the back of his neck stand up. She was now on autopilot, and there was no stopping her. Jess solemnly nodded, turned, and walked over to Bear. Without a word, she snatched one of his Bowie knives out of its holster. Jess knew it would be razor sharp because Bear always kept his weapons in tip-top shape and ready for immediate action. Plus, Bear loved the Bowie knife; another gift from the Earth-based United States military machine. Turning back to the warden, she held the knife up.

"Um, Captain," Max said, his voice wavering. Eps just looked at him and shook his head.

"You don't scare me, Smythe," the warden cackled.

"I don't want to scare you," she said, a giddiness in her voice. "I just want my sister." Once again, she was met with silence. Abruptly, she stuck the knife down his pants up to the hilt. With a swift pull, the knife easily sliced through his belt, pants, and down to his undergarment. Without any material to hold them up, they dropped to the floor, leaving the warden exposed from the waist down. The guards collectively gasped. Taz let out a low squeal. Max cringed, while Bear and the marines looked at each other with big smiles, expectantly waiting for some gore. Before the gasps subsided, Jess had the business edge of the knife, at the hilt, pressed up and under the warden's scrotum, forcing the warden up on his tiptoes.

Eps had to give him credit. He never flinched or uttered a word during the whole altercation.

"I'll ask you again, nicely," Jess said, coldly, as she applied more upward pressure. "Where's my sister?" Dead silence filled the hall and the cells. All the inmates were craning for a view of what was going down.

"You wouldn't," the warden croaked out. He went higher on his tiptoes. Beads of sweat started down the sides of his face.

"Don't try me."

"Epsilon, this is quite unprofessional! You need to control your pet!"

Eps took several steps toward them. Jess glared at him and he stopped in his tracks. "Actually, Warden, if she were my pet, I certainly would control her. But, you see, she isn't. The real problem for you, is that you took someone special from her. I strongly suggest you give her what she wants. And I wouldn't dally."

"Yes, I took her," the warden said, with an evil smile. "And her flower was a most delightful delicacy."

With a loud grunt and all her might, Jess pulled the knife up and toward her. The razor-sharp blade sliced cleanly through, severing the warden's manhood from his body. It fell to the cold stone floor with a resounding 'plop,' that echoed loudly in the silent cavern. The warden's face drained of color as his brain finally comprehended what just happened and he let out a blood-curdling scream. Within minutes, all the blood drained from his body and he slumped over, dead. Three of the guards threw up. Max crossed his legs and winced. Eps closed his eyes. Even though Taz had seen her fair share of gore, she had to turn away and suddenly realized, again, that she really had to pee. Bear and the marines still had that "shit-eating" grin on their faces, just eating up the vision.

"Okay," Jess continued, holding the bloody knife up. "Who's gonna tell me where my sister, Maggie Smythe, is?" Several of the guards started to cry, mumbling that they didn't know who she was or where any girl named "Maggie Smythe" was.

"I...I...I n...n...know where she is," the guard who had pointed out Papu said. "Some of us are just simple villagers, made to work as guards, under the threat of our families ending up here if we didn't. Please ma'am, don't hurt us."

"You know where my sister is?"

"Yes, ma'am. I can take you to her."

"What is your name?"

"Athlin, ma'am."

"Okay, Athlin," Jess said, as she wiped the knife on the dead warden's shirt and walked over to Athlin. She cut the bindings holding his wrists. She turned and walked over to Bear and started to put the knife back in its holster.

"Whoa," Bear said, grabbing her wrist and stepping back. "That'd be yours now; I don't what that nastiness back."

"Oh, you're such a wuss," Jess taunted, as she broke free from his grasp. She kept the knife in her hand and turned back to Athlin. "Lead the way."

Athlin walked over to another guard and Jess pressed the knife into his back. "No, no, it's ok," he said. "I need the keys." He held up a ring of keys he took from the other guard. Jess removed the knife from his back and Athlin started off for the opposite door.

"Max and Bear coordinate with the rest of the Marines, liberate the prisoners," Eps said. He was met with cheers and whistles from the inmates. "There is a village about five klicks to the north. We'll rally there and figure out what to do with them."

"Roger that," Bear said. They trotted off to start releasing prisoners. Eps caught up to Jess, Taz, and Athlin at the far door.

Athlin was nervously fumbling with the keys, trying to find the right one. His hands were shaking so bad he was having trouble getting the key into the hole.

"Easy, there," Taz said, putting her hand on his. "Relax. No one is going to hurt you, I promise." She looked directly at Jess while she was talking. Jess stood there with a blank look on her face, patiently waiting for the correct key to unlock the door. Athlin finally opened the door, and they all walked through and entered a stone corridor. They were already several levels below the main complex. The corridor was dimly lit and twisted several times before it merged into a larger tunnel. They followed this tunnel several meters and ended up at a large door, similar to one you would find on a cargo bay. Selecting another key, Athlin inserted it into a panel next to the door and twisted. With a low-pitched rumble and a loud screech, the large door opened. As they walked through the door, the stench hit them, all at the same time. Athlin threw up. Taz recognized the smell as decaying flesh.

"You said you were taking me to my sister," Jess roared, grabbing Athlin by the throat and putting the tip of the knife under his jaw.

"Stand down, Commander," Eps ordered, as he grabbed Jess's wrist. "She's right there." He pointed to the top of a pile, and sure enough, there was Maggie. She was lying naked, on top of other corpses, discarded food, and assorted trash and debris. They had walked into the complex's garbage disposal area. The pile was in the middle of a pit. The nearest pit wall looked like a giant plow with three large pistons attached to it and going into the deck they were standing on. Once the pit was full, the pistons would extend, and the plow would move the contents into an opening along the opposite wall. Once the material was inside, lasers would vaporize the contents.

Jess let go of Athlin and lowered the knife. "I'm so sorry," he said, tears soaking his face. "I liked Maggie. She was really nice to us, despite all that was happening to her. She kept saying her big sister would come for her."

Jess barely acknowledged him and started for the pit, tears

streaking down her cheeks. Eps still had a hold of her wrist and pulled her back. She whipped around and looked at Eps like she was going to start spitting nails at him; but she never raised the knife.

"I'll get her. I have a much better chance of surviving whatever bugs are in that pile." Jess relaxed and dropped the knife on the floor with a clatter that reverberated in the stone chamber. She finally broke down, audibly sobbing. Eps let go of her wrist and she fell to her knees, hunched over. Eps turned to Athlin. "Take off your shirt and pants."

"Huh?" Athlin was confused.

"What part of strip down didn't you understand?" Jess yelled at him, in between sobs. He immediately stripped down to his underpants and handed Eps his clothes as ordered.

"Thank you," Eps said, as he took the clothes and turned toward the pit.

Jess stayed where she was, crumpled, crushed, and crying. *Eps was right; she's dead.*

Athlin started to follow, but Taz stopped him, bent down, and picked up the knife, and handed it to him. "Get out of here," she said, softly. "Go free your other villagers and go home."

"Thank you." He trotted off toward the door and stopped when he reached it. He turned around, gave a half smile, half grimace, and disappeared through the door.

Epsilon had already entered the pit; squishing sounds came from under his boots. He continuously swatted flies, and other strange looking bugs out of the way. As he neared Maggie, crunching noises became more prominent as he stepped on and snapped bones, producing an unbelievably gut-wrenching sound. Finally reaching her, he picked up her lifeless, naked body. Even in death, he couldn't help but notice what a beautiful girl she was. He immediately had a flash back to the time he first met her when Jess invited him to spend leave with her and her family. He never expected to see her like this. Jumping back to reality and fighting tears himself, he pulled Athlin's pants over her scrawny legs and buttoned them up around her waist; there was a lot of room left. He put her atrophied arms through the shirt sleeves and started to button the shirt over her emaciated torso when he thought he saw her chest rise slightly. Staring at her bare chest, he put his ear up to her mouth.

"Reginald!" Jess yelled, indignantly. "What the hell are you doing?"

*Yes!* Maggie's chest fell, and he felt the slightest warm, moist breath hit his ear. Straightening up, he grabbed Maggie and yelled, "She's alive!" He ran toward the edge of the pit, not caring what bones he was crushing under his boots as he ran. All that mattered was getting Maggie to Taz. Taz would save her. He got to the side of the pit, and both Jess and Taz had their hands out. He handed Maggie to them and they laid her down on the cold rock floor. Taz scanned her as Eps hoisted himself out of the pit and ran to her side. *Come on, Maggie!*

"Holy crap!" Taz exclaimed. "She has a faint pulse and some brain activity, but it's fading fast. It doesn't make any sense."

"Yes, it does," Eps said. "I touched her bare flesh."

"I don't understand."

"Move out of the way and stand back." He pushed Taz away and put one of his hands on her forehead and the other on her chest above her left breast and closed his eyes. The silence in the cavern was deafening. All of a sudden, his hands started to glow. Moving lines of light could be seen flowing down from Eps's arms, through his hands, and into Maggie. Color started to drain from Eps's face. Maggie started to gasp and breathe.

Taz was mesmerized. *Oh my god. Eps has the power to share his life force. Wait, he's not sharing it! He's giving it!* Taz snapped back to the present. She fumbled with her medical scanner and finally started scanning Maggie and Eps. "Jess, he's giving his life force to her."

"No, he's not," Jess said. "He's sharing it to help repair the damage to Maggie's body."

"No, I'm telling you he's giving it to her. But it isn't working. As fast as her body is being repaired, it's degenerating. It's no use. She's too far gone for his healing power to work.

They're both going to die!"

As much as Jess loved her sister and felt it was her fault that Maggie ended up here, she didn't hesitate in her decision. "I'm not going to lose you both today!" Jess shouted, as she ran full force at Eps. She collided with him and knocked him off of Maggie. They both rolled on the floor with Jess coming up on her feet. Eps just laid there on this back.

Taz was at his side, instantly scanning him. "He's in serious shape. I don't see his body repairing itself. I need to get him to sickbay."

"Smythe to *Stingray*," Jess said, into her communicator.

"Crash here," barked the communicator.

"Lock on to us and beam us directly to sickbay."

"Aye, Commander."

\* \* \*

The four of them materialized in *Stingray*'s sickbay. Crash had put Eps in one bed and Maggie in another. Taz was busy attending to Eps. Both women were forced to forget about Maggie and were focused on Eps. A gasp behind them stopped them in their tracks. They turned to see Maggie looking at them, eyes wide open. Taz and Jessie looked at each other in bewilderment. "Go to her," Taz said, softly. "You have your chance to say your goodbye."

Jess went to Maggie's side. "Mags."

"Jessie," Maggie faintly croaked out.

"I'm so sorry. This is all my fault."

"Don't blame yourself. It's okay. I love you, Jess."

"I love you, Mags." Jess was crying, tears falling on Maggie's hand that Jess was holding.

"Tell Reggie I...." She never finished the sentence. Her pupils dilated, and she let out her last breath.

"NO!" Jess yelled, as she bent over and put her forehead on Maggie's hand. "Taz, do something!"

Dr. Zubreé put her hand on Jess's shoulder. "I'm sorry,

Jess. There's nothing I can do. There's nothing anyone can do."

The communicator on the wall beeped. "Bridge to sickbay. I need the Captain on the bridge immediately," Crash announced. Jess made no move to get up.

Taz walked over and hit a button. "The Captain can't come right now."

"Then I need the Commander on the bridge right away."

Taz looked over at Jess, who was still bent over Maggie. "She's on her way. Taz out." She killed communication and walked over to Jess, took her by her arm and pulled her up. "You are needed on the bridge right now, Commander Smythe!" she said, firmly, as she whipped Jess around to face her. "You're in command now. You need to snap out of it and focus! There will be time for this later."

Jess looked at Taz numbly. "You save him!"

"I will. And I will take care of your sister. Right now, WE need YOU! Go!" Taz led Jess to the door and pushed her through.

* * *

Jess entered the bridge. "Status!" she barked, as she sat down in the command chair. Crash was at his station, and Bear was at her normal station.

"Eight CMC cruisers dropped out of hyper-space at the opposite edge of the system," Crash said. "I think it's the sixth fleet, but I'm not sure. They tried a few times to hail the prison. A few minutes ago, they started towards us but abruptly stopped and returned to their original position. They've been holding there ever since. The prison has been evacuated. Only the guards are still secured in there. Max and some of the Tenoderite marines finished their final sweep and are at the village."

"Bear, target the prison complex, full plasma cannon spread, total destruction."

"Aye, Commander," Bear said, as he punched buttons on his console. "Complex targeted."

"There are still people down there," Crash said.

Jess ignored him. "Fire!" Bear hesitated. "Is there a problem, Chief?" Jess was on her feet.

"No ma'am. I thought maybe the Commander would like the pleasure of pushing the button, ma'am."

Jess relaxed and sat back down, though, still a bit irritated. "No, Bear, there is no pleasure in killing. Now fire!"

"Aye, Commander, firing," Bear said, and pushed the fire button. Three shimmering purple blobs of light left *Stingray*'s underbelly at one-second intervals and headed for the planet surface. Each blob of plasma impacted the prison complex at strategic points and erupted into huge fireballs, emitting a blinding purple light. A mushroom cloud two kilometers tall and one kilometer in diameter emanated from each impact site and blended together to form an ominous-looking structure. The resulting shock wave vaporized everything in its path for two kilometers out from the combined epicenter. Everything for the next two kilometers instantly erupted in flames. The remaining trees in the final kilometer coming up to the village, were knocked over and by the time the shock wave hit the village, it was little more than a strong, hot wind. Some windows were shattered, and anything not tied or staked down was blown over.

When the dust and smoke settled, there was nothing left of the prison complex but an enormous crater. The heat was so intense that it turned the first few inches of dirt into smooth glass that shimmered in the smoky haze of the sun shining on it.

The fires would continue to burn for four days. Two torrential rainstorms would not be enough to put them out. The crater was so hot that the rainwater instantly turned to steam, and it would take a full two weeks before any water would collect in it. During the next two months, Mother Nature reclaimed the land up to the crater, sprinkling it heavily with vegetation and fauna. Within a year, the crater filled with rainwater and became a lake. Assorted fish and other water-dwelling life-forms spawned and called it their home. The new forest and lake would serve as a fertile hunting ground for villagers and wildlife alike.

"Commander," Crash said. "Incoming message from—

Conglomerate One—" he turned to Jess. "It's the President, ma'am."

"This ought to be fun," she said, solemnly. "On screen." The image of President Amabo materialized on the screen.

"Lt. Smythe," Amabo started.

"It's 'Commander' now," Jess interrupted.

"I stand corrected, Commander. I need to speak with Captain Epsilon."

"MISTER, President," Jess responded with a slight nod and as much disdain in her voice as possible. "The Captain is not available right now and, as such, I am in command. There are eight of your warships standing ready to enter this system. I swear I will destroy each one of them if they attempt an approach."

"Commander, I have personally ordered them to hold their current position. Let me take this opportunity to offer my condolences for the loss of your parents."

"'LOSS' of my parents? More like, you killing them and my sister too, while we're at it!"

Amabo dropped his head and lost his "salesman" smile. "Yes, you are entirely correct. It has recently come to my attention the unauthorized use of power, influence, and official assets by Admiral Roth. I'm also aware that the illegal use of force resulted in the deaths of your parents and other inhabitants of their village."

"And my sister!"

"Well, Commander—"

"Don't even go there!"

"You are correct. Your sister's death was a result of Roth's actions and, as such, I ordered his arrest. Roth is in custody and will stand trial for his crimes."

"Like that means anything."

"Oh, don't be so down on the Conglomerate justice system," exclaimed Eps hoarsely, as he slowly walked on the bridge. Jess noticed he was still quite pale as she got up and stood next to the command chair while Eps settled into it.

"Captain Epsilon," Amabo said.

"Mr. President," Eps responded with far less drama. In

reality, he was just too damned tired to make a big fuss.

"Captain, one of our ships is an aid vessel. I would appreciate it if you would allow it to approach and render any assistance to the refugees that is needed."

"The village could use a lot of humanitarian help, as well."

"We are willing to provide it. In light of the atrocities I've just been advised of that have been going on there, it is the least that we can do. We are also willing to take the refugees and re-locate or re-unite them with their families."

"How do I know you won't just take them and throw them in another jail?"

"You have my word on it."

"Which means what?"

"I understand your doubt Captain, but I am looking you in the eye, man-to-man, and promising you they won't be."

Eps thought about it for a moment. "Okay, vessel approaches at one-half sub-light speed. Any attempt to raise shields or to power weapons and I'll let my XO use it for target practice, understood?"

"Agreed. I'd like you to turn over *Stingray* to the captain of the CMC *Kardon*. Again, I promise you and your crew safe passage to wherever you want to go."

"Not on your life, Mr. President. Any attempt to take her will be met with overwhelming force."

"I don't want *Stingray* falling into the wrong hands, Captain."

"Neither do I, and she won't. And you have MY promise on that. Good day, sir." Eps severed communications. "It will take the *Kardon* two hours to traverse this system. Where is Admiral Rhys?"

"He's in the village square," Crash answered.

"Jess you're with me. Crash hold down the fort."

## CHAPTER NINE

Eps and Jess materialized in a very crowded village square. There were lots of beings milling around. Most of them were human, but there were a few three-headed Corgons and several Oti. The Oti were lizard people. They were one of the first species to join the Alliance and the last one to fall. It was a fierce battle; their home world was virtually destroyed, and they were now considered extinct. Some of the villagers, who were human, and the Tenoderite marines were tending to the wounded. Eps and Jess located Admiral Rhys and approached. He was talking with Prince Papu and, what appeared to be, the village elder. An Oti female had her arm interlinked with the Prince's. "Your Highness. Admiral."

"Captain!" Rhys exclaimed. "I'm glad to see that the rumors of your mortal injuries were exaggerated."

"Me too. Listen, there are eight CMC warships at the edge of the system. One is inbound to render aid and re-locate the refugees."

"I know," Rhys said, smiling at Jess. "I heard that you have one feisty XO here. If you ever decide to leave our good Captain, my lady, you are most welcome aboard my flagship."

"Thank you, Admiral," Jess said, with a smirk. "But I assure you, I'm quite content where I am."

"Anyway," Eps resumed, "I think you should depart with haste, Admiral. I don't want the Conglomerate getting a look at you."

"You are correct. Colonel, round up the troops and transport back to the ships." The Colonel saluted and walked off.

"Captain," Prince Papu said. "I'd like you to meet Samantha, my cellmate during my time in prison. She is most beautiful, don't you agree?"

"Yes, she is, Your Highness," Eps responded. Samantha blushed. Well, as much as a lizard could blush, anyway.

"She kept me alive. The guards didn't know what I was or what I needed to eat. She took several beatings for me. Eventually, she convinced the guards to let her make meals that I could eat. Turns out the Oti and the Tenoderites share a biological symmetry. Mostly the villagers who were enslaved as guards took pity and responsibility for my welfare. Over time, I gained the respect of the humans. Most of you are kind."

"Well, Your Highness, unfortunately a few bad apples spoil it for the rest of us." The prince gave him a puzzled look.

"Captain," Samantha spoke up for the first time. "There are a few of us that would like to return with Prince Papu to the Tenoderite home world. We have no families left. No friends. Nowhere to go."

"With your permission, Captain," Prince Papu took over. "We will welcome anyone from here who would like to live with us. You have my word that they will be treated fairly, like any other Tenoderite citizen."

"Same for us," the village elder said. "Thank you for liberating our brothers and sisters, mothers and fathers, sons and daughters from those heinous overlords."

"Permission is not a power I wield," Eps said. He turned to the group that congregated around Samantha as they fell silent. "You are all free to make your own decisions. You decide whether to go with the CMC and try to regain your past lives, stay here, or go with the Tenoderites."

The former prisoners started talking amongst themselves, deciding which path to take. A small group formed near the Tenoderites, a larger group headed into the village, while the third equally large group stayed in the center of the village square to wait for the CMC cruiser to arrive.

"Commander Smythe," Papu said, as he gently took Jess's hand in his claw. "It has been a pleasure meeting you and my sincerest condolences on your loss. I, unfortunately, did not get the privilege of meeting your sister. However, I did hear through other prisoners that she was indeed a remarkable soul." He kissed her hand. The little hairs around his mouth tickled.

"Thank you, Your Highness." Jess was truly touched by his kind words.

"Captain," Rhys said, "I bid you farewell—until next time our paths cross."

"Hopefully under better circumstances," Eps responded. They shared a hearty embrace; again, an awkward sight to witness. Eps stepped back and then the Tenoderites were gone in the flash of the transport artifact. Eps turned to the village elder. "The *Kardon* should be here shortly. We will be watching to make sure they don't pull a fast one. If I were you, I'd press them hard to leave as many provisions as you think you will use and need."

"Yes, Captain," the village elder said. "I do believe that to be a wise suggestion. Thank you again."

Eps nodded as he called Crash on his communicator to beam him, Jess, and Max up. They, too, were gone in the flash of the transport artifact.

* * *

"Sitrep!" Eps barked, as he, Jess, and Max entered the bridge and assumed their stations.

"Tenoderite cruisers high-tailed it out of here," Crash answered. "The *Kardon* is on approach, one half sub-light, no shields, weapons safe, sir."

"Roger that. Break orbit and lay in a course for the *Kardon*, one-quarter sub-light."

"One-quarter sub-light, aye."

"Commander, get me the captain of the *Kardon*."

"Aye," Jess said, as she brought the image of the *Kardon's* captain on screen.

"I am Captain Rogers, command CMC *Kardon*," Rogers said, nervously.

"Captain, I am Captain Epsilon, command *Stingray*. Please proceed to the planet. I implore you to leave plenty of provisions and supplies for the village. Their population has increased substantially."

Rogers appeared to ease a bit. Eps could tell, the good captain didn't like this anymore than he did. "Those are my orders. You are on a direct collision course, please change course."

"No funny business, Captain. I'll be watching." Eps severed communication. The image of the *Kardon* replaced Rogers on the screen and the ship was fast growing in size on the screen. "Crash, heading change, zero-nine-zero degrees."

Crash quickly executed the course change before acknowledging. "Course changed, zero-nine-zero degrees, aye Captain."

"Jump to hyper-space and then double back. Cloak once you secure from hyper-space, then park us in orbit of the closest moon."

"Aye Captain."

* * *

From *Stingray's* vantage point, everyone on her bridge had a bird's-eye view. The *Kardon* settled into orbit. Several shuttles departed the *Kardon* and headed to the village surface.

"Scanning the shuttles," Jess announced. "Sensors indicate they are laden with supplies, sir. Also, a half-dozen armed marines."

"Sounds like a small security force," Bear chimed in.

"That's what I'll assume," Eps said. "Keep an eye on them, Bear."

"Aye, Captain," Bear affirmed.

"Captain," Jess said. "I have a single shuttle departing

*Kardon* with a crew of four. They are now at the prison site and scanning the area; moving to the remote communication site and scanning again; now they're returning to the *Kardon*."

"That's odd," Max said.

"They wanted to see what *Stingray* was capable of," Eps said. "Now they know."

* * *

It took the better part of six hours for the *Kardon* to ferry the mammoth amount of supplies the President promised and return the refugees to the ship; all the while, under the watchful eye of *Stingray* and her crew.

"That's that last of the shuttles," Jess announced. The screen showed the *Kardon* break orbit, turn toward the other CMC warships waiting at the edge of the system, and jump to hyper-space. Simultaneously, the remaining seven CMC warships disappeared; they too jumped to hyper-space, their mission here finished.

"Crash, lay in a course for Varguti, wave power five," Eps said. He put his elbow on his chair's side rail and buried his face in his hand, but not before noticing that Jess was missing. He was pretty drained.

"Course laid in for Varguti," Crash said. "Wave five, aye, sir."

Another commotion below decks wafted up through the open bridge hatch and jolted Eps. Bear and Max got up, but Eps waived them off as he started toward it. "No, stay put, I got it." When he got down to the bottom of the ladder, he saw Taz standing defensively in front of sickbay, clutching a tablet hard against her chest. Jess, red faced, was standing mere inches from her. "Ladies, take it down a notch."

"I want to see it!" Jess screamed. Taz nervously looked at Eps, who put his hand on Jess's shoulder. The gesture seemed to relax her, and she took several steps back. Taz noted that Eps seemed to be the only one that could 'get to' Jess. There was some sort of obvious chemistry there, even if the two of them didn't want to admit it. Eps gave Taz a slight nod.

Relieved that she didn't have to make this decision, Taz consulted the tablet. "As you presumed, I performed an autopsy on Maggie. She actually died of Diggersococcus dwarf pox virus, or more commonly known as Diggers Syndrome."

"What the hell is that?"

"It's an airborne pathogen that enters the body through the lungs. Usually humans can fight it off, unless there is a lesion, or cut, in the lung. She had evidence of a recent tear in her lung, near a previously fractured rib."

"Last time I saw her, we were horsing around, Maggie and I—she tripped and slammed her side into the edge of a table—she started spitting up blood...," Jess's voice trailed off.

"Well, that would explain it. The broken rib punctured her lung. There was a lot of scar tissue around it and with all she's been through, some of it probably separated, just enough to let the bug in. With her being malnourished, well, her body had no chance to even put up a fight.

"The virus usually lives in a fruit called a marple and it's actually beneficial to the Alterians, as it aids in their digestion. *Their* stomachs are impervious to the virus. Eventually, the virus dies from the acids and is passed out of their bodies normally. We humans have a much higher acid level in our stomachs then the Alterians do, so the virus dies even faster, within seconds of entering our stomachs. The problem arises because the virus is close to the skin of the fruit. It can become airborne and inhaled by the person eating the fruit. That's why the Alliance restricted marple imports so they can only come into one specific port. However, the Conglomerate, realizing the profits being lost by this added step, turned a blind eye and marples started turning up at other ports. Those ports weren't equipped to irradiate the fruit.

"The first symptom is a cough for a few days. If detected within the first few weeks of being infected, it can be successfully treated."

"But prison protocol is to screen anyone with a cough; they

don't want an epidemic to break out in the prison population," Eps thought aloud.

"Yes. But Diggers is really rare. You must be looking for it and have the right equipment to detect it. Prisons don't have any of that. If not caught, it literally eats you from the inside out. It starts with the blood-laden organs and then the destruction worsens exponentially. It attacks the less vital organs first and by the time it does enough damage to cause death, it's been several agonizing months for the victim. That's why Eps couldn't save her. The damage was far too great and there were so many bugs, they were causing damage faster than he could heal her. Had we gotten to her months ago, I could have saved her, Jess. I'm so sorry."

Jess chuckled. "She survived all that, just to be taken out by a bug." She shook her head in disbelief.

"If it's any consolation, I found a fair amount of an opiate derivative in her system. They were giving her the real stuff for the pain, not the synthetic crap that hardly touches this level of hurt. Based on the residual amount still in her system, I believe she died in relatively little discomfort. Somebody cared for her."

"What did they do to her, Tamson?"

"Jess, the disease is what she suffered from and ultimately what killed her. Leave it at that." Jess coldly glared at Taz. Taz nervously glanced at Eps, who gave the slightest nod. Taz looked down at the deck and let out a sigh. Gathering herself, she looked back up and directly at Jess. "There was evidence of pelvic bruising and vaginal tearing." Jess never wavered; her eyes locked with Taz's.

Eps knew all along Maggie would have been raped (and probably gang-raped). But hearing Dr. Tamson Zubreé say it out loud, felt like someone rammed their fist right into his gut. He closed his eyes, hoping this was just an awful nightmare. He hoped that when he opened them back up, Maggie would come bounding out of one of the doors to give him a great, big hug.

"How many times?"

"Jess—"

"How—many—times?"

Taz looked at Eps. He opened his eyes and they, too, were full of hurt. He, again, gave a slight nod. Jess deserved to know what her sister went through. "It's hard to tell, but I would say multiple times. Unbelievably, I only found one foreign genetic sample inside her and that matched the lone genetic sample I found deeply embedded in her fingernails."

"Who?"

Taz didn't bother to look for Epsilon's approval. "The Warden."

Jess chuckled. It gradually built, and her laugh continued until soon, she was near hysterics with tears streaming down her face. She buried her face in her hands but couldn't stop laughing and crying at the same time. "Oh, how apropos that I cut his dick off!" She continued to laugh uncontrollably.

Eps nodded for Taz to scram, which she did, without hesitation, and headed up to the bridge. She was glad to let someone else deal with the grieving family; that was the part of being a doctor that she hated. Eps took Jess in his arms, burying her face into his shoulder. He held her tight with his left arm and stroked her hair using his right hand. There was nothing he could say to comfort her. There was nothing he could do to make the hurt go away. He had to let her cry it out. At that moment, Captain Reginald Epsilon realized that he was powerless; he didn't have a solution. *I always have a solution.* He also came to the realization that he loved them both. Who knows what could have blossomed with Maggie if the opportunity arose? Who knows what might happen with Jess if she stayed with him? If he would let her stay with him, this time. *I'll outlive her, just like I outlived Talia. Oh Talia.* That brought back a flood of memories. His first love ended many decades ago. She was the love of his life. She stood by him all those years as she grew old and he didn't. Eventually, they would have to move to a remote area where no one would see the drastic age difference. Oh, the pain when he had to bury her. *It wasn't fair to Talia. It won't be fair to Jess. I can't let her get close. But I want to—what am I going to do?* "Come on, Jess. Let's go say goodbye to Mags," he said, snapping back to reality. He guided her through the door and into sickbay. Maggie, fully covered with a sheet, was still lying in the bed, a shimmering containment field around her. Eps switched it off and turned down the sheet, just enough to expose Maggie's face. He took her left arm out from under the sheet and held it. Jess put her hand on top of Maggie's and they both held her, and each other's, hands.

Eps bent over and kissed Maggie's forehead and whispered, "Goodbye Mags. Rest in peace. I'm sorry. Love you." He slid his hand out, put it on Jess's shoulder and squeezed. He kissed her on the top of her head, then turned and left sickbay, leaving Jess alone with her sister.

## CHAPTER TEN

"Assuming standard orbit around Varguti, Captain," Crash announced. Everyone was on the bridge except Jess and Taz. "We're being hailed."

"On screen," Eps said. An image of an old man filled the screen.

"I am Tran, Keeper of Varguti," he announced.

"I am Captain Epsilon."

"Unfortunately, Captain, we have been expecting you. I take it you have the younger Ms. Smythe with you?"

"Yes."

"To be interred?"

"Yes."

"That is most unfortunate, as we had hoped otherwise. We have prepared a spot for her, next to her parents. I've enforced a large, restricted-access perimeter around the graveyard to keep the...fuss...to a minimum."

"The 'fuss'? What the—" Taz blurted out, as she entered the bridge on the tail end of the conversation.

"Captain Epsilon's reputation precedes him. Most of our citizens feel it is his fault that so many of our innocent people fill our graveyards. Your presence here will cause grief, protests, and, potentially, lead to mayhem. However, out of respect for our dearly departed, the young Ms. Smyth has a right to be interred in her native land. A right that we take very seriously."

"We'll be quick, Keeper, and shan't dally," Eps said.

"I sincerely appreciate it. With Ms. Smythe's permission, I will grant the requests for access to a handful of relatives of the departed, as well as several close Smythe family friends. Where is Ms. Smythe?"

"She is—as you can well understand—in private meditation. On her behalf, I give you permission to authorize the access requests. I'll trust your judgment in this matter."

"Of course, we don't want an incident. Oh, and as per protocol, I, too, will be in attendance. Unless that does not meet with your—er—Ms. Smythe's approval."

"That's fine. I look forward to meeting you in person, Keeper Tran."

"Yes—likewise—the feeling is mutual. Please proceed at your convenience." Tran severed communication.

"What the hell?" Taz exclaimed. "It wasn't your fault, Eps. Holy crap!"

"Easy, Tamson, simmer down. I know that. You know that. If it means peace for the Smythe family, then so be it. I'll take the heat."

"Take the heat for what?" Jess asked, as she came on the bridge. Everyone clammed up.

"Nothing...," Eps said. "The main reactor was showing a higher than normal heat level. Max is on it. Anyway, Keeper Tran advised that they are awaiting our arrival. Taz, is Maggie ready?"

"Yes. I fashioned a dress out of some material I found in one of the crates in the cargo bay. It's not much, but she looks nice."

"Thank you Tamson," Jess said, teary eyed. She gave Taz a big hug.

"Crash helped me; I couldn't manage her by myself. But I dressed her, so she wasn't...you know...."

"It's ok. I appreciate it." She hugged Crash, too.

"Right then," Eps said. "Gentlemen, if you would escort Maggie to the surface." The guys all nodded and headed down to sickbay to get the coffin. "Taz, if you would go with them and…well…make sure they don't drop her, or just plain screw it up. I'll bring Jess down."

"Of course," Taz said. She gave a reassuring smile as she looked from Eps to Jess and headed out.

They stood there for a few quiet moments; their eyes locked on each other's. "Come on," Eps finally said to Jess. He gently took her by her arm and guided her down the ladder. They arrived in time to see the three guys moving Maggie's coffin on an anti-gravity sled out of sickbay and into the cargo bay, for transport to the surface. The door closed behind them, leaving Eps and Jess alone. They stood in silence for a long time, just looking into each other's eyes.

"I can't believe she's gone," Jess finally said.

"I know."

"It's not your fault, Reg."

"It's not your fault either, Jessie."

"I know. But I'm her big sister. I was supposed to protect her, not put her in harm's way."

"If anybody 'put her in harm's way,' it was me. I shouldn't have let you stay with the Alliance. I really thought, by going into hiding—abandoning everyone—it was the safest route for all."

"They still would have taken her."

"I should have brought you all with me."

"And what, live on that desolate planet?"

Eps didn't have a response. They stared deep into each other's eyes for a while, inching closer and closer to each other. Eps found his hands on her waist, and Jess rested her hands on his shoulders. They could feel the heat radiating off of each other; their breath gently caressing each other's lips. Jess closed her eyes and licked her lips as they came close together, almost touching.

The door to the cargo bay slid open and Crash appeared. "Um—oh—wow—didn't mean to interrupt—but, they're ready. He turned red with embarrassment and looked away.

Eps pulled back and cleared his throat. "Okay—not interrupting—thanks, we'll be right down."

Crash turned and retreated. As the door closed, Eps and

Jess could hear him mumble, "Not interrupting, yeah right, that's not what the bulge in the Captain's pants was saying…."

Jess instinctively looked down. She turned crimson, and a slightly shy smile graced her face. "Mmm," is all she said, as she turned and headed after Crash.

Eps followed. *Oh boy!*

* * *

Eps and Jess materialized in the graveyard, a few meters from Maggie's grave. Her coffin was still on the anti-gravity sled above the hole in the ground. Taz, Crash, Max, and Bear were gathered around. A bit behind them, but back enough to discern an evident, empty space, was a throng of people, presumably relatives and family friends. Eps could see what Tran meant earlier. There were dozens and dozens of heavily armed security forces creating a perimeter to keep back the onlookers, several of them carrying signs with not-so-nice things written on them. He could hear them chanting and yelling. They were too far away to make out what they were saying, but he surmised it wasn't complimentary. To most, Epsilon was a hero. But here, he was the devil. He was the reason Jess's parents were dead. The reason her sister was dead. And the reason so many other Varguti citizens were dead. Never mind that they all died at the hands of Conglomerate soldiers. Their reasoning: if Eps didn't do what he did, the soldiers would never have come in the first place. They were right. But they were also wrong. Allowing the Conglomerate to get stronger would mean a tighter reign, less freedoms, and more strong-arm tactics. Unfortunately, with revolution, comes sacrifice and Eps paid the highest price. Not by his life being sacrificed, but the lives of people he loved being sacrificed. The lives of people he didn't know, innocents, being sacrificed. And the most expensive, the life of one dearest to him, having to endure the pain of losing her entire family. All because of him and his actions. *Why does Jess remain so fiercely loyal to me?*

Several people approached Jess as they walked toward the

gravesite. Eps slowed his pace, giving Jess her own space and grief. She hugged several of the people. He thought he recognized a couple from pictures in the house when had visited last: aunts and uncles, if memory served.

Keeper Tran approached and shook hands with Jess. He totally ignored Epsilon. *That's okay; it's part of my punishment.* Instead, Eps joined the rest of his crew around the coffin.

"It is nice to meet you, Ms. Smythe," Tran said. "My heartfelt condolences to you. Your parents were wonderful people. And Maggie—such promise—so vibrant, full of energy."

"Thank you, Keeper," Jess said.

An awkward silence ensued. "Well, unfortunately, I could not find a minister who was willing to perform the ceremony," Tran continued, with as much sincerity as he could show. "I'm terribly sorry, such a disgrace to the Belief."

Jess wasn't buying his sincerity. "That's okay. It's a function that a ship's captain can perform. I know Captain Epsilon would be happy to fill in." The color drained out of the Keeper's face.

*Well, it's a shame that their religious and political leaders were too busy with being politically correct instead of doing the right thing.* "I'd be honored," Eps said. He knew this was Jess's passive aggressive way of telling the Keeper to shove it, politely, of course. Deep down, though, Eps believed Jess was relieved to have him say a few words, instead of some stranger.

"Okay, let's get this over with," Tran said. Jess was ready to strangle him.

*Stingray*'s crew and the Keeper gathered around the coffin while the rest of the friends and relatives stood off at a slight distance. Eps positioned himself at the head of the coffin, cleared this throat, and directed his comments toward the friends and relatives standing behind. "Whatever you think of me or the politics of what happened; this is a personal time of mourning. For the family's sake, please come and join Jessie." Relief washed over everyone's face, and hesitantly, one or two of the townsfolk stepped forward. The rest followed and soon, all were gathered around. While Eps waited, he caught Jess's eye, and she smiled. Surprisingly, he noticed that the crowd of onlookers quieted, and the signs were dropped. "Right. I wasn't as fortunate as most of you were to know Maggie as well as you did. I can say, from the short visits when I met her while on leave, I took an immediate liking to her. What wasn't to like? She was young, full of energy and enthusiasm, beautiful, had so many plans and ideas for the future. I know it's disheartening, and it makes you angry—makes me angry—that her life was snuffed out, way before her prime. It doesn't matter how or why. What matters is that we remember the 'how' and the 'why' she lived. How she made all of us feel when we were around her: Alive. That was her gift...." For the second time in his long life, Eps was overcome with emotion—mostly guilt. "I'm sorry." Eps had to turn away. Her death and his inability to save her tolled hard on his soul. He always saved 'em. He always won. He lost this battle and it hurt.

Jess stepped up. "I will always remember my sister's innocence. She looked at everything with the naivety of a child. Sometimes, I thought she did it on purpose, just to get a rise out of everyone around. She would giggle after you explained it to her. That is what I will miss the most. I love you Maggie, may you rest in peace." She put a local Seelia flower on top of Maggie's coffin.

A commotion at the foot of the coffin immediately brought Eps out of his funk and his hand drifted to his weapon. A man in robes was pushing his way forward. Bear and Max immediately drew their weapons, prepared for a fight. "My apologies," the man huffed and puffed, "Lady Jessie." Evidently, the jog from the perimeter was a little too much for the portly fellow. It only took a moment for him to finish catching his breath. As he stooped over, he held his hand up for everyone to wait a minute. Straightening up, he continued. "I'm Minister Fami from the Order of Twelve. Your family belonged to my order. Lady Maggie deserves a proper Vargutian burial. The Captain was correct; politics should play NO part in The Mourning," Fami glared at Tran. He turned to Jess, "May I?" He looked nervously to Bear and Max.

"Yes, please," Jess answered. Bear and Max holstered their

weapons.

"I take it the eulogy is over?"

"Yes," Eps said, relieved.

"Excellent." Fami motioned to two other robed individuals who were standing, unnoticed and flanked by two armed soldiers, well behind the group. They started forward, each carrying a basket, with their escorts in tow. The mourners parted and allowed the two newcomers to join the minister.

One of the soldiers approached Keeper Tran and in a low voice said, "They're clean, sir." The Keeper gave a dismissal nod. The two soldiers did an about-face and returned to the perimeter.

Minister Fami removed the flower Jess put on top of the coffin and gingerly returned it to her. "At the proper time," he quietly said. She nodded. "If everyone," he continued, "would take a handful of petals in each hand." He motioned to the other robed assistants who offered their baskets to the mourners. As instructed, everyone took handfuls of petals. Minister Fami mustered his sing-song preacher voice and raised his hands to the sky.

> *"Oh, King Of The Universe Above, filled with mercy and residing in the Great Beyond, bring proper rest beneath the wings of Your Heavenly Presence.*

> *"In the midst of the lines of the holy and the pure, cast your light like the sun burns bright upon the soul of our beloved Lady Maggie, who went to her eternal place of rest.*

> *"May you, who are the source of mercy, eternally shelter her beneath your wings, and unite her soul among the living that she may now and forever, rest in peace.*

> "And let us say: *Amen.*"

"Amen," everyone answered back.

Fami tossed the petals from his right hand on top of the coffin. "My friends; please approach the Vessel Of Afterlife and release the petals from your right hand on top of it." Each one in attendance approached the coffin and emptied the petals from their right hands on top of it. Fami continued. "Lady Jessie, please cast off your loved one to the Great Beyond."

Jess approached the coffin, and once again placed the flower on top. "Go and be at peace. Kiss Mom and Dad for me."

"Will the bearers please place the Vessel Of Afterlife in the ground." Max expertly manipulated the anti-gravity sled remote, and the coffin lowered into the ground. "Rest, my weary one," Fami said. He stood over the hole and dropped the remaining petals from his left hand. "Lady Jessie, if you will." Jess walked over, tears streaming down her cheeks and emptied her left hand into the hole. Fami placed his hand on her shoulder to keep her at the edge. "All in attendance, please cast the remaining petals into the earth." Everyone approached and cast their petals into the hole. "It is customary to cover the vessel, Lady Jessie first." Fami indicated toward a traditional, metal-bladed, wood-handled shovel that was sticking out of a pile of dirt. Jess walked over and grabbed the shovel, sticking it in the dirt and coming up with a mound. She walked over to the grave and poured it in atop the head of the coffin. She returned the shovel to the dirt pile. "Are there any blood relatives of Lady Maggie present?" Two aunts and two uncles approached, along with several cousins. "It is important to return the shovel to the pile and not hand it to the next mourner, thus not transferring your grief to the next mourner." They each grabbed the shovel, filled it with dirt, poured it atop the casket, returned it to the pile, then hugged and kissed Jess. There was not a dry eye among the mourners. Keeper Tran lost the fight, openly bawling like a baby. Even big, bad Bear couldn't hold the tears back.

As the last cousin finished, Jess grabbed Epsilon by the hand and led him over to the pile. Pre-empting the minister, she said, "Eps, please."

Eps needed no urging. He manhandled the shovel, scooping up the dirt, but then gingerly poured the contents on top of the casket. "I'm sorry, Maggie. Please rest in peace."

Jess motioned to the rest of the crew of *Stingray* to do the same. "You are my family now." Taz, Max, Bear, and Crash took turns putting a shovelful of dirt on the casket.

"If anyone else would like to pay their respect to Lady Maggie, please step forward," the minister announced. Each of the townsfolk, including the Keeper (it would, of course, be an unwise political move to not partake) took turns putting a shovel of dirt on the casket. "May the King Of The Universe Above, go with you and yours in peace."

"Amen," everyone joined in. Without any words or looks, the townsfolk headed back to their homes. The minister looked over to Max and nodded. Max and Bear got busy using the automated excavators they brought down from *Stingray* to fill in the remaining portion of Maggie's grave.

The protesters were still there, waiting to see what the Demon Epsilon (as was written on one of the signs) would do next. Eps hoped, in his heart of hearts, that the hate was directed solely at him and none of it at Jessie, Maggie, or the rest of their family. That is what he would believe. He would bear it for Jess. He would give up his own life if it would bring them all back.

"Minister Fami," Jess said.

"Yes?"

"Thank you for stepping up and conducting a proper burial. It would have meant the world to Maggie. And it meant a great deal to me."

"It needed to be done." He turned to face Eps. "My apologies for usurping your authority, Captain."

"No apologies necessary, Minister," Eps said. "You are the authority in these matters. I, too, am glad you stepped in and it was conducted properly. Maggie deserved that."

"Well then," Keeper Tran butted in. "It would be best if you took your leave. The protesters and all."

Jess turned to him and in the most seething voice replied,

"Thank you for 'allowing' us to bury my Vargutian sister. However, I intend to pay my respects to my parents' grave before I 'take my leave.' If that is a problem, you can kiss my ass!" She trotted off toward her parents' graves. A stunned Keeper looked at Eps.

Eps saw that Bear and Max were finished filling in the grave. "Max, Bear, Taz, and Crash return to *Stingray*. I'll collect Jess and return in a few minutes."

"Aye, Captain," Crash said.

"Thank you, Captain, for your cooperation," Tran said.

Eps stared icily at him but held his tongue.

"Um," Tran continued, "take your time." He trotted off toward the perimeter.

Eps turned and went to join Jess. She was putting Seelia flowers on both graves. He put his arm around her, and she leaned her head into him. "We have about as long as it takes the Keeper to make it to the perimeter and order the commander to come and arrest me."

"You mean 'us.' If I hadn't joined the Alliance Of Arms over everyone's protests—" she said.

"That has nothing to do with any of this. However, they probably will try you as an accomplice."

"I just wanted to say goodbye to my mom and dad. Tell them the next time I see them will be when it is my turn to go to the Great Beyond." She turned and looked up at him. "Promise me you will lay me to rest here, with the rest of my family."

"It would have to be covert."

"That's ok."

"You're not afraid of what they would do to your grave when they found out?"

She chuckled. "Vargutian custom and law forbid any tampering with grave sites."

"But—"

"Vargutians are steadfast about their customs, no matter what the circumstances are. No grave has ever been vandalized or robbed, no matter how controversial the deceased was."

"I promise."

"You'll be arrested if they catch you."

"I guess I'll have to be careful not to get caught."

She smiled as she extended up and kissed Eps quickly on the lips. In doing so, she noticed, over his shoulder, that the Keeper was talking to the brigade commander and pointing to them. "Time to go, Eps."

"Right." They disappeared in the transport artifact.

# CHAPTER ELEVEN

Eps and Jess joined Crash on the bridge. "Two Vargutian patrol ships are flanking us, Captain," Crash said. "They are politely requesting our departure schedule."

"Ignore them, Crash," Eps growled. He'd had enough of their political crap. "Lay in a course for the Vista Colonies, wave two."

"Aye, Captain," Crash said. "Course laid in, breaking orbit. Let's rattle their cage a little bit. Full sub-light, he he he."

"Just don't hit 'em, Crash."

"What, me?"

"Captain," Jess interrupted the boys. "Oh, never mind, it's gone now."

"What was it?" Eps asked.

"I thought I had a heat signature of a CMC vessel, but my mind must be playing tricks on me."

"Hmm. Crash, momentary slow to wave one point five, like the engines faltered," Eps said.

"Slowing, mark. Resuming wave two," Crash said.

"THERE!" Jess exclaimed.

"What's going on?" Max asked, as he bounded up on the bridge. "My engine just bucked."

"It's CMC all right, Captain," Jess said. "Scout class. I think she's the *Napoleon* but can't be sure at this range. She's running at ninety percent on her reactor, which is why I can see her that far away. She's generating a hell of a heat signature." Scout class vessels were smaller, extremely fast ships, the fastest in the Conglomerate arsenal. The trade-off for the speed came at the expense of the hull and weapons; she had to lighten her load and, as such, she presented a much smaller profile to prying sensors, giving her the ability to get closer to the enemy without being spotted. While she could fend off a strike or two with her shields, that was about it. Her weapons were weaker than that of a normal star cruiser, so her fight back capability was quite limited. Her assignment was probably the most dangerous: gather up close and personal intel on the enemy. Her defense: turn and run, as nothing could catch her. Except *Stingray.*

"We're too far away for them to see us," Max said. "We are well beyond CMC sensor technology."

"I agree," Eps said. "Otherwise, they would have detected our momentary drop and countered by dropping back as well. Commander, bring up our course on the NAV."

"Aye Captain," Jess said, as the star map appeared on the main screen with *Stingray's* course shown by a fat, blue line.

"What's that off to the right, there?"

"It's a space whirlpool; basically, just a bunch of space debris and asteroids rotating around an impromptu gravitational well."

"That'll work. Crash, subtle course correction to that debris field."

"Aye Captain," Crash responded. "Course has been corrected. Should be on target in two hours."

"Captain," Jess said. "Enemy vessel has changed course, still in pursuit, maintaining distance."

"How can they follow us if we are outside their sensor range?" Taz asked. She and Bear had come on deck a few minutes into the current conversation.

"We've been tagged," Eps surmised. "That's the only explanation."

"Impossible," Crash said. "I ran a security sweep when we came on board. If we were transmitting, I would have seen it on the security monitor."

"What if someone came on board while we were on Varguti?" Taz asked.

"*Stingray* is securely locked when we leave the ship. Even if the CMC had transport capability, *Stingray's* shields would have activated to disallow transport. We can transport because we have the proper code. Same thing with the airlocks; they're secured."

"Nevertheless," Eps said, "I want a ship-wide sweep by hand. Jess, Max, Bear, breakout the portable scanners. Stem to stern. I'll handle the bridge."

"Aye Captain," they all said, while grabbing portable scanners and heading off.

* * *

It took the better part of an hour, but the entire ship was scanned by hand. The crew reassembled back on the bridge.

"Sitrep!" Eps said.

"Clean," Bear said.

"No traces of any transmitter or signal," Max said.

"I got nothing," Jess said.

"This doesn't make any sense," Taz exclaimed.

"Actually—it—does," Max said, softly. All eyes turned to him. "It's a focused beam. We'd have to be between it and the receiver to pick it up with our scanners."

"But you've been all over the ship. At some point, one of you would have had to have been in between them."

"Not necessarily. It is obvious the transmitter is sending to the ship that is BEHIND us. Therefore, the transmitter has to be tagged to the trailing most edge of *Stingray*, on the outside, and pointed away from us. We'd never know it was there."

"How do we find it and get it off?"

"Anyone up for a spacewalk?" Eps asked.

"Not while we're in wave drive," Taz responded. "You'll be torn apart."

"Correct. Jess, how far behind are they?"

"Once we drop out of wave, we'll have sixty minutes; ninety tops if they detect we've stopped and slow."

"Good. Crash, when we arrive at the debris field, pick the largest object and put it between us and that ship. The signal should be interrupted, causing a little confusion on their end and give us some added time. I'll take a shuttle out and scour the rear edge to see if I can find it."

"There may be more than one," Max chimed in.

"Good point. Once I locate them, Jess will beam Max and Bear out to that point to remove it. Let's suit up."

\* \* \*

Max and Bear donned space suits and were standing on the transport platform, with Jess at the controls. Eps jumped into the shuttle and strapped himself in.

"Eps to Crash," Eps said, over the COMM.

"Crash here. Dropping out of wave, now. Standby." Crash found a large asteroid, about twice the size of *Stingray,* and maneuvered her behind and close to it. "Okay, Captain, opening the bay door and you are ready for launch."

"Copy that." Eps started the shuttle and flew her out the open door. He turned to the right and headed straight for the tall point of the port side wing. He activated the scanner on the shuttle, and it lit up like a Christmas tree. "Found it, top point of the port wing. Want to bet there's another one on the starboard wing too?" Eps saw Max and Bear materialize at the top point of the wing as they secured themselves to it. Eps continued scanning down the wing, made the turn to starboard, continued to scan along the aft edge of the ship, turned up and finished at the tip of the starboard wing. Once again, the scanner lit up. "I win. I win. I found another transmitter on the starboard wingtip." Eps headed back over to where Bear and Max were trying to remove the first transmitter.

"This thing is not secured with a magnet," Bear mused.

"We could have picked up the magnetic field, if it was," Max replied. "Looks like some sort of adhesive. Whoever did this knew what they were doing. Bear is going to try to pry it apart enough for me to get a laser cutter in there and cut the adhesive." Everyone could hear Bear grunting and straining as he slipped a crowbar in between the wing and the transmitter and pulled. "It's not separating. You have to pull hard, Bear."

"What do you think I'm doing?" Bear asked, indignantly. "You want to switch places?"

"No, I'm not as strong as you, just smarter."

"Grrr!"

"Okay, it's separating a little." Max activated the laser cutter and touched it to the adhesive. It cut through like butter, and the transmitter started to separate. The bar gave suddenly, and Bear lost his balance, tumbling out into space.

"Ahhh," Bear yelled. The tether line caught him, so he didn't fly away into the vast beyond.

"Okay, got it. Let me clean the rest of the adhesive off of the wing. What should I do with it, Captain?"

"Hold on to it," Eps answered. "Attach your tether to the shuttle and I'll drag you over to the other wingtip." Eps maneuvered the shuttle close and Bear attached the tether to the shuttle.

"Captain," Crash interrupted, "confirmed enemy vessel is the *Napoleon* and is still inbound. You have less than thirty minutes."

"Copy that," Eps said. The shuttle was now at the starboard wingtip, and Bear secured the tether to the wing. Bear shoved the bar in between the wing and transmitter and pulled. Max wasted no time getting the laser cutter on the adhesive. This time, Bear was ready for it to give and didn't lose his balance. Max cleaned up the wing.

"Okay, now what?" Bear asked.

"Max," Eps said, "give the transmitters to Bear." He did. "Jess, beam Max back in." Max disappeared in the transport artifact. "Bear, you ready for some space acrobatics?"

"Bring it!" Bear responded.

"Attach your tether the shuttle and hang on."

"Ready."

Eps slowly moved the shuttle around the asteroid, hugging its surface to minimize the possibility of detection by the *Napoleon*. He positioned it on the opposite side of *Stingray* and smack dab in the middle. "Bear, attach the transmitters to the face of the asteroid and make sure they point straight out."

Bear let go of the wing he was holding onto and gently pushed off toward the surface. The tether caught him. "I need about a meter and a half closer, Captain."

"Roger that." Eps gently moved closer to the surface.

"That's good." Bear cut two square holes in the rock and fit the transmitters into them. Then, he pulled on the tether and returned to the shuttle. "All done, Captain. Let's get out of here."

"Captain," Crash said, "the *Napoleon* is slowing. They must have reacquired the signal and detected that we stopped."

"Roger that," Eps responded. He had the shuttle at the bay door. "Jess, beam Bear back in. It's too dangerous to drag him in on the shuttle. Crash, as soon as we are in cloak and put us at a good vantage point."

\* \* \*

The three guys headed straight for the bridge after returning to *Stingray*. Epsilon settled in the command chair. "We are thirty kilometers above and one thousand kilometers into the debris field, Captain," Crash reported. "We should have a bird's-eye view from here, sir."

Right on cue, the *Napoleon* dropped out of hyper-space. After a moment, she turned and proceeded to the asteroid that had the transmitters on it.

"Think they figured out they've been had?" Max chuckled.

"Yes," Jess answered. "They just sent a message to Command advising that we figured out we were tagged, and that they lost us." The *Napoleon* backed out of the debris field, stopped, and held her position.

"Why haven't they left yet?" Taz asked, after a few

minutes.

"It's like they're waiting for something. They aren't scanning."

"They're not waiting for something. They're waiting for someone," Eps remarked. "Crash, put us nose to nose with her."

"Aye, Captain." Crash maneuvered *Stingray* in front of the *Napoleon* so she filled up the forward screen.

"Crash, de-cloak. Commander, hail the *Napoleon*."

*Stingray* de-cloaked as the image of the *Napoleon* was replaced with an image of her captain. "I am Captain Sophia Ziggy, command CMC *Napoleon*," Captain Ziggy said.

"I had a feeling you were on that boat," Eps said, with a smile. "Congratulations on your promotion, Captain."

"Thank you, sir. My XO didn't think you were still here."

"But you learned well and knew better."

"Unlike Jacobs, I valued my stint under your command on the *Freedom*."

"I'm a little surprised to see you playing for the wrong team."

Ziggy leaned forward, her face filling up the screen. Eps detected the slightest wink. "Just trying to survive, Captain; just trying to survive." She leaned back.

"Aren't we all?"

"My helmsman was emphatic that we turn and run when you de-cloaked. I explained to him that it would be futile since we couldn't outrun you."

"True. But you also couldn't turn and jump to hyper-space before I put a laser bolt right up your tailpipe."

"Touché. I also remember the lesson of realizing when your goose is cooked, you accept it."

"But have a backup plan."

"Oh, I have a backup plan. So here we are. What's your next move, Captain?"

Eps was impressed at the calm coolness Sophia exhibited. She certainly learned well. He knew one day she would make a fine Alliance officer and a great Captain. "I know you do. Well,

Captain, it's your lucky day and your backup plan will work. I have no intention of obliterating your ship and your crew. Your helmsman will have the opportunity to turn and—calmly drive away."

"That's comforting to know."

"However, there is one thing I would like you to do." Ziggy raised an eyebrow. "Tell your overlords they won't get *Stingray* back. And I won't be as nice the next time I meet a CMC vessel chasing me and planting devices on my ship."

"I will relay it."

"Oh, and while you're at it. Tell them that they should all resign, disband the Conglomerate, and return rule to the individual planets."

Ziggy chuckled. "Really? You think they'll *ACTUALLY* listen."

"Tell them I'm putting them on notice. Goodbye, Sophia. It was good seeing you again."

"Likewise, Epsilon."

Eps severed communications and the screen returned to showing the *Napoleon*. She turned, sped off, and jumped to hyperspace. The bridge fell silent.

"What was her backup plan, Captain?" Bear asked.

Eps got up and headed to the door. "She knows me. Everyone assemble in the mess in fifteen."

Bear had a perplexed look on his face.

"If Eps knows you," Jess answered Bear's unasked question, "he'll give you the benefit of the doubt. Unless you've given him a reason not to."

\* \* \*

Eps entered the cargo bay and walked over to one of the walls. He touched a panel, and a drawer slid out. He rummaged through it and finally pulled out a small treasure chest. He found this chest on an abandoned ship, clutched in the arms of a long dead pirate. The ship had been picked clean well before he stumbled upon it. The raiders left the chest behind, figuring it had no value. He claimed it as his bounty, so he couldn't count the trip as a total bust. It would come in handy at some point down the road, he figured.

* * *

Carrying the chest, Eps walked into the mess hall and dropped it at the head of the table with a thud. Jess, Tamson, Jimmy, Max, and Bear were all seated and talking amongst themselves, but stopped when Epsilon walked in.

"Right, then," Eps said. "I want to thank each of you for your help in rescuing Maggie, even though it didn't turn out as I had hoped it would."

"Yes," Jess chimed in. "Thank you. Your help meant the world to me. You risked a lot for someone you didn't even know." Taz rubbed Jess on her back. She knew it was hard for her to talk about this.

"We know you," Crash said. "That's all that matters. Besides, you'd do it for us."

Eps opened the chest. "In all my travels, I haven't had a finer crew." He pulled out maroon-colored, velvet bags stuffed full with gold coins. Even out in space, gold was the universal currency and commanded immediate purchasing power. He handed a bag to each crew member as he spoke. "I know that what you did to help Jess out, is what friends do for friends, but this bag represents a small token of my appreciation."

"No, no, I can't take this," resounded around the table from everyone.

"Yes, you can. And you will need it," Eps responded. Puzzled looks were on everyone's face. "We're going to resume course for the Vista Colonies. They're neutral ground. The Conglomerate signed a treaty to stay out of their sector and not harass any of their ships. So far, it appears that they have honored that treaty. You will be able to blend in and from there you can secure transport to anywhere you wish to go."

Bear broke the silence. "You're gonna scuttle *Stingray*," he said, matter-of-factly. "Aren't ya?"

"What does that mean?" Taz asked.

"It's an old nautical term," Crash answered. "When ships floated on water, to scuttle her meant to take her to deep water and blow a hole in her keel, or bottom, so she'd sink to the ocean floor. In modern times, it means to take her to an empty part of space and blow her up, totally destroying her."

"NO!" Taz yelled. "You can't destroy *Stingray!*"

"I can't let her fall into Conglomerate hands, Taz," Eps said, solemnly. "We just witnessed that they will stop at nothing to get her back. She's an awesome weapon and in the wrong hands, she can unleash unbelievable devastation."

"But in the right hands, she can do so much good. And she won't fall into Conglomerate hands. Not with all of us aboard protecting her!"

"The Conglomerate won't stop hunting us down until they get her. All of you will have a better chance splitting up and blending in."

Taz was all fired up now, her china white skin taking on the same flame color as her hair. Everyone around the table involuntarily sat back, fearing she might whack them in their heads as her hands were flailing about as she spoke. "Splitting up? Blending in? What, you think I could just waltz into, oh I don't know, say Mayo Clinic on Sivad and ask to be put on staff? Conglomerate security would grab me in a heartbeat."

"Taz is right," Max chimed in. "We have nowhere to go. No one to go to. There's no place we can go that we can blend in." Silence ensued.

"Besides," Taz snarked, visibly calming down, the redness draining from her face and her skin returning to its normal beautiful paleness. "One thing I learned during this exercise is that the safest place in the universe is right behind Captain Reginald Epsilon." Everyone laughed, even Eps smiled.

Jess got up, faced Eps with a stern look, and crossed her arms in front of her. "Wherever you go, I go. I'm not leaving you this time; not no way; not no how; whether you like it or not."

Eps started to say something, but Jess just glared at him. He knew better than to argue with her when she got something set in her mind.

Max got up. "Yeah, what she said. I'll be in the engine room if anyone needs me. But since you insisted, I'm keeping the gold." He gave a big, toothy grin and hustled out.

"I'll be in my quarters cleaning my gun and sharpening a NEW Bowie knife, no thanks to the Commander," Bear said, as he grabbed his bag and trotted out the door.

"I'll be in sickbay...um...rearranging meds," Taz said, as she exited and flashed a quick grin at the duo.

Crash was the last one to get up. "Course, Captain?"

"Pilot's discretion," Eps answered, never taking his eyes from Jess's.

"SWEET! I know this cool planet with lush exotic jungles, hot chicks, waterfalls, sandy beaches, plenty of libations...," his voice trailed off as he bounded out of the mess and up the ladder to the bridge.

The door closed, leaving Jess and Eps alone. "See what you started," he said.

Jess smiled and moved toward him. Eps could feel *Stingray* change course. She bunched up the zippered edges of his leather jacket in her fists. His heart started to pound. He resolved to himself that at some point, he would have to give in to her. He had no choice. *I love her. I can't fight it. But I have to fight it.* She looked up at him for what seemed like an eternity. *I'm scared; for her and for me.* "Jess—" he whispered.

"Shh," was all she replied as she put her index finger on his lips, still looking up at him. She pulled his lower lip down and curled her finger. He readily took it in his mouth and sucked on it a little bit. Jess let out the slightest moan, their eyes locked on each other's.

Eps realized that he had his hands on her mid-section and squeezed ever so gently. *She's so soft, for such a tough cookie.* She closed her eyes as she let out another slight moan.

"Eps—" she started, but never had the chance to finish, for at that moment, *Stingray* violently lurched, a sickening sound of metal grinding on stone broke their trance.

Instinctively, Eps grabbed Jess as they were thrown across the mess hall. He twisted his body, keeping her on top of him, so he fell first to the floor, cushioning her fall. The force of flying across the room, coupled with Jess's weight on top of him, broke three of his ribs as he hit the floor and opposite wall. "AHHH!" he yelled, a split second after they both heard the bones snap.

When they finally came to rest, Jess was still on top of Eps, pain evident in his face. "CRASH!" they both bellowed in unison.

"Sorry, Captain," Crash said, over the ship-wide COMM. "Didn't see the asteroid."

THE END
(for now)

Join Captain Reginald Epsilon and the rest of *Stingray*'s crew as the saga continues…

### *Stingray: Prophecy*

*It is written that in the kingdom of Castianis's darkest hour, with the queen on her deathbed, their defenses failing, and chaos reigning outside, the Prophecy begins: A man and a woman fall from the sky; the goddess Sophina reveals herself to a young princess and guides her to a reunion with the brother she never met; and a seed is planted for the future of both kingdoms.*

*Three worlds collide around Captain Reginald Epsilon as he comes face-to-face with his arch nemesis Sir Severin Greymoor. Severin has been planning this encounter for a long time, and it is not going quite to plan. Dr. Zubreé finds true love and is willing to give up everything to be with her new beau. Commander Jessie Smythe fights to keep Stingray from being destroyed by Greymoor's drones while following Epsilon's trail. What she finds along the way will test her and Epsilon's blossoming relationship.*

*Can the crew of Stingray keep themselves together while desperately trying to save the kingdoms of Castianis and Danerana from falling into a complete meltdown?*

I would like to take a moment to say "Thanks!"
for purchasing this book.

Your support means a lot to me!

I love to stay in touch with my fans.

Please sign-up for my newsletter:
http://subscribe.GaryZeiger.com

You can follow me on Social Media:
Just click one of the "Follow Me" buttons at:
http://GaryZeiger.com